The
Summer
I Got
A Life

For
Kevin and Eric

The
Summer
I Got
A Life

Mark Fink

WestSide Books ✐™
Lodi, New Jersey

Published by WestSide Books
60 Industrial Road
Lodi, NJ 07644
973-458-0485
Fax: 973-458-5289

Library of Congress Control Number: 2009930791

International Standard Book Number: 978-1-934813-12-6
School ISBN: 978-1-934813-28-7
Cover design by David Lemanowicz
Interior design by David Lemanowicz

Printed in the United States of America
10 9 8 7 6 5 4 3 2 1

First Edition

The
Summer
I Got
A Life

1

Get Me Out of Here

I was totally pumped! There are only so many times in your life when you feel like that. Maybe hitting the winning home run in the bottom of the ninth. Or being the thirteenth caller on K-ROCK and winning a new iPhone. I wouldn't know. Those things never happen to me. So for now, the last day of school is as good as it gets.

Don't get me wrong, I don't hate my high school. It's just that after 174 grueling days, enough's enough. Okay, so it wasn't exactly 174 days. I missed two with pink eye, six because of the flu, and one because my brother got his hand stuck in the toilet. More on that genius later.

The bell rang at three, and the kids in Earth Science let out this humungous roar. They stormed the door and almost trampled our poor teacher. When I looked back, I saw him with his hand on his head, trying to keep his toupee from flying off in the draft of the departing students. The minute I stepped into the hallway, it hit me: that once-a-year disease had struck again. It was time for the Last Day of School Syndrome. Everyone had the same stupid grin, and they were laughing, crying (well, some of the girls), signing yearbooks and being obnoxiously nice. Kids were actually hugging people they wouldn't be caught dead with yesterday.

That's the part about high school that really sucks; it's a social minefield of groups, labels, and cliques. And you navigate them at your own risk.

Here's how it works at my school:

At the top of the food chain, you've got your Very Cool. These are the jocks, the cheerleaders, the rich kids, and, of course, the really good-looking, those freaks of nature who have perfect skin and could have their own MTV show in a heartbeat.

The next group is the Almost Cool. They hang with the Very Cool when they're allowed, but mostly they're just a bunch of wanna-bes.

Then you've got your Semi-Delinquents. They're the kids who get into just enough trouble to be popular, but somehow avoid getting suspended.

Finally, on the bottom of the food chain are the geeks, the criminals, the foreign exchange students, and the really, really stupid.

The trick is to try to fit in somewhere, but this isn't as easy as it sounds. Now, I'm certainly not Very Cool. I'm not even Almost Cool. I don't have the guts to be a Semi-Delinquent, and luckily, I'm not a total geek, so I don't fit into that category. I really don't quite fit anywhere at all. Instead, I, like, blend into the walls of the hallway and practically disappear.

But on the last day of school, everybody's your friend. So I signed a few yearbooks, shook a few hands, and had almost made it out of there alive when I suddenly heard her sweet voice.

"Hey, Andy." It was Kimberly Willis, co-captain of the cheerleaders. I turned around to see if there was another Andy she might be talking to, but I was the only Andy in the hall.

This was a first. I could hardly believe that this hot girl, the coolest of the cool, only a bus crash away from being head cheerleader, was actually talking to me. In three years, the only words this goddess had ever said to me were "You're standing on my foot, dweeb!" We were doing the Virginia Reel in phys ed, and somebody pushed me into her.

Without blinking, I came back with the wittiest thing I could think of.

"Hey, Kimberly." How lame was that?

"So, what are you doing this summer?" she asked.

I knew the answer to this one, and I couldn't wait to tell her. "I'm going to Hawaii," I said, trying to be nonchalant, like I was going to the 7-Eleven.

"Cool," she said, flashing a smile with the straightest, whitest teeth I had ever seen. I was on a roll, so I decided to keep going.

"Are you doing anything this summer?"

"Yeah, I'm going to Switzerland." And when she said it, it *did* sound like she was going to the 7-Eleven. Now, there's nothing wrong with Hawaii, but Switzerland, man, that's in Europe! How do you top Europe? But like an idiot, I tried.

"Our hotel pool has a 50-foot water slide." *The Acad-*

emy Award of lame. The second it came out of my mouth, I wished a bolt of lightning would strike me dead. Kimberly started laughing, and it wasn't a kind laugh, either. And in case she had any doubt about what a tool I was, the voice bellowing down the hall took care of that.

"Crenshaw, are we walking home together, or what?"

That would be the voice of Darryl Knott, and there's no way any guy can be cool when he's walking home with him. His legal name was Darryl Knott, but most people called him Snot, and for good reason. Snot was the most allergic guy on the planet and had severe allergic reactions to 36 different things—including his own mother.

Darryl was always sneezing, coughing, wheezing, and gasping. His nose was always, like, running, and the running often was more like gushing. He tried to catch the flood with tissues, but that was like trying to wipe up the Amazon with a kitchen sponge.

To give you the total picture, Darryl wore two MedicAlert bracelets and carried three different inhalers. He tucked one into his sock, the way movie gangsters hid their extra guns.

As you've probably figured out by now, nobody wants anything to do with Snot. But I guess that's one reason I like him. Okay, I admit I kind of feel sorry for him, but there's more to it than that. When you actually get to know him, Darryl's a pretty good guy. He's honest, smart, funny, and loyal.

When Kimberly heard Darryl's voice, she slammed her locker and took off down the hallway like she was running away from a fire. She might talk to me only once a year, but she does have her limits even then. At least I got to step on her foot once. That's more than most guys can claim.

So Darryl Knott and I walked home from school for the last time that year. After a few sneezes and a couple of shots from his inhaler, Darryl told me his summer plans. He'd visit his grandmother in Sacramento and then spend a week at the Mayo Clinic in Rochester, Minnesota, where he would see yet another allergist. My summer was looking better all the time.

2

Brad

The minute I opened the front door, that hypnotic smell hit me. Piled high on a plate, the chocolate chip cookies were calling out to us. But when Darryl leaned over for a whiff, he erupted with a huge sneeze. At least he turned away from the cookies. Unfortunately, he zapped a pan of meat loaf. I made a mental note to avoid it at dinner.

As we sat eating our snacks, I heard grunting from the backyard. It meant my brother Brad was home, which also meant no peace. I looked out the window, and there he was, sprawled across his weight bench, lifting a barbell that would've crushed me in a heartbeat. And Brad, as usual, was sweating. He's the only one I know who actually sweats when he reads. Of course, for Brad, reading is heavy lifting.

✸

Brad's seventeen—two years older than I am, or, as he constantly reminds me, exactly 800 days older. His real name is Bradley, but whenever I call him that, he smacks me.

I'd like to say we have one of those typical love-hate brotherly relationships, but lately it feels more like hate-hate, and mostly coming from Brad. The older he gets, the less he wants me around. He won't let me hang with his friends, and he won't let me anywhere near his room. But this is no great loss—it smells really bad in there.

Brad's sole mission in life is to be both cool and "a total babe magnet," and he spends every waking minute working toward those goals. He's, like, obsessed with his body, his tan, and especially his stupid hair. He spends so much time in the bathroom, I suggested that he move his bed in there. Somehow, he didn't find that amusing.

In this world of awesome technology, Brad's favorite invention's still the mirror, and I mean *any* mirror. I swear I've even caught him checking his hair in front of the toaster. I've busted him endlessly on his hair obsession, too, even telling him once that hair mousse causes cancer. That cost me another smack, but it was worth it.

Brad's a pretty hard guy to live up to in most ways, and that's part of the problem between us. He's got Dad's good looks, and girls just seem to cling to him. And to prove that life isn't fair, Brad's also a major jock. He's starting point guard on the high school varsity team, a two-year baseball letterman, and an all-state wrestler. Now, how does a skinny guy like me, with no major talent to work with, compete with an older brother like that? Sure, Mom says I have a gift for words, but I'd trade that in a heartbeat to have Brad's killer jump shot and his looks. Like I said, when it comes to being fair, life sucks.

But there is one thing I've got on Brad: I'm way

smarter than he is. He'll never admit it to me, but somewhere, deep down under that tan, he knows it as well as I do. Some of my happiest times are when he needs me, especially for help with his homework.

Here's how it goes down: he comes into my room looking sheepish and then asks me how I'm doing. That's when I know I've got him. "Need some help with something, Brad?" I once rewrote his Civil War term paper, and he had to pay me 20 bucks. When he ended up with an A–, it was one of the proudest moments of my life.

Besides those few times when he needs my help with homework, Brad's pretty much a jerk. He teases, bullies, or ignores me, which is probably the worst of all. But then, about a month ago, it happened. He got his first car. Now he's more of an asshole than ever, because he's my ride to school and *that* really pisses him off. "I didn't get a car to be your personal chauffeur!" he says as he's driving. I tell him to keep his eyes on the road. And true to form, he smacks me.

⁘

A few minutes after I got home, Brad walked into the kitchen—big surprise—sweating. "Hey, kid. Hi, Snot." Then he opened the fridge and drank right out of the juice carton.

"That's so disgusting," Darryl groaned.

"Disgusting? Snot, you should know. You're the poster child for disgusting."

"Leave him alone, Brad," I said.

"Hey, you tools, want to play some B-ball?"

Not really, I thought. But Darryl answered for me, before I could open my mouth.

"Sure!" he exclaimed, all excited.

"No thanks, Brad," I said.

"Come on," Brad pleaded, "you two against me. We'll play to 20, and I'll give you guys 14. If you beat me, I'll drive you anywhere you want."

"You're on, big guy!" Darryl leaped out of his chair, banging his knee on the table.

As Darryl limped out and I followed him into the yard, I had that familiar sick feeling in the pit of my stomach. These stupid games always led to trouble, and Brad dominates me in any sport he wants. Strong and quick, he darts around me, shoots right over me, or muscles me into the garage door. And I always end up bruised, bleeding, or both.

There was one magical day when I beat him: it was September 25, 2005. Brad was fooling around, taking fancy shots. But I was really on fire, sinking every shot I put up. When the score got too close, Brad tried harder to win, but by then it was too late. I managed to hit a wild 20-footer and ended up winning by two. Brad didn't talk to me for two days—possibly the best 48 hours of my life so far.

But now the game was on. Brad gave us the ball so we could warm up and watched us from a lounge chair. Darryl took a shot from the free-throw line, and it missed the rim by three feet. Darryl sucks at basketball. In fact, he sucks at almost everything except chess.

Darryl missed another shot badly.

"Oooh, I'm in trouble now," Brad mocked.

Obviously, I'd have to be the go-to guy here. So I huddled up with Darryl for a quick game plan: "Okay, try to play defense. Get a rebound if you can, and try to stay out of my way." Darryl nodded and slapped me five. Then he blew his nose on his T-shirt.

"You girls can take it out," Brad said as he threw a hard chest pass that glanced off my head. The game hadn't even started, and I was hurt already. Darryl took the ball out, and I dribbled toward the hoop, feeling good—until Brad stole the ball with a flick of his hand and was gone.

"Stolen by Crenshaw!"

That was the worst part of these games: Brad also had to announce. He dribbled the ball between his legs, blew past me, and practically jumped over Darryl's head for an easy layup. "What a move by Crenshaw! We're in for a treat today, folks. Wimps 14, Crenshaw 2."

The next time we had the ball, just as Brad got on me, I whipped a pass to Darryl. Although it knocked the inhaler out of his pocket, he held on to the ball and launched an ugly shot that bounced on the rim forever but then finally fell in. Darryl was more surprised than anyone, and he began to scream, but it came out more like a wheeze.

Brad, still in sportscaster mode, described the action his own way: "Snot hit a shot! Snot hit a shot! Asthma Boy has scored, believe it or not!" We now led Brad 16-2. Two more baskets and we'd win.

Brad took the ball out and hit eight straight jumpers from all over the driveway. "Crenshaw from the top of the key, yes! Crenshaw from the baseline, two more! This is one of the most amazing displays of shooting I've ever seen!" It *was* pretty impressive, even with only me guarding him.

We were now down 18-16. Brad needed one more shot to win. He was still laughing as he dribbled to the top of the key.

"Stop him, Andy—do something," Darryl pleaded.

"I'm doing everything I can." That's when I came up with it—a brilliant defense that had never been tried before, not by Jordan, Magic, Bird, or Kareem. I was about to make defensive basketball history, right there in my very own driveway.

Brad stopped dribbling 20 feet from the basket. The way he was shooting, this shot was a sure thing. I was right on him, but then I backed off a few feet.

"Bet you five bucks you don't make this shot," I dared him.

"You're on, Mini Me. But you know you can't foul me."

"I won't even have to touch you," I promised.

As Brad went up for his shot, I whirled around and pulled down my shorts, mooning him before he could flick his wrist for the shot.

He was so shocked he fell backward onto his butt—as the ball flew out of his hands and straight into mine. Darryl and I burst out laughing, and after Brad's face returned to a normal shade, he was laughing, too.

Now it was my turn to announce: "An incredible defensive play by Andy Crenshaw! It's the Full Moon Defense, and it's definitely put a crack in Brad's confidence!"

Darryl was laughing so hard he started to cough. But then he started to choke, and he seemed to be having trouble breathing.

"Shit. Maybe we should do CPR," I said.

"I'm not putting my lips on Snot."

"Fine, I'll do it. Is it four breaths and two compressions, or two breaths and four compressions?"

"You're asking me? You know I suck at math."

"Is he looking a little blue to you?" I asked.

"He always looks a little blue to me."

By now, Darryl *was* gasping for air, and he was pointing to something on his left.

"I think he wants his inhaler! Get his damn inhaler, Brad!" I shouted.

Brad ran over and picked it up, then bent over Darryl and sprayed two quick bursts. But Brad had the nozzle turned backward and ended up spraying himself instead.

That's when I grabbed the inhaler and shot a couple of bursts into Darryl's gaping mouth. Luckily, he started breathing normally again before we managed to kill him.

"Thanks, guys. You really saved my life."

"It's the least we could do," Brad said.

Darryl was better, but he sat and watched while Brad and I finished the game. My brother hit a rainmaker from the end of the driveway to win, but by then, nobody cared. Brad congratulated me on my inspired defense.

"Dude, that was the funniest thing I've ever seen on a basketball court." No matter what, I always could make him laugh.

3
Life Sucks

Only two more days! In less than 48 hours we were going to Hawaii, to the island of Maui, to be exact. Once again, I checked out websites for Maui and saw pictures of its best beaches. We'd be staying in a condo just steps from this awesome beach on the Wailea side of the island. I could hardly wait to get there.

Even though I'd have to share a room with Brad, it was still going to be great. I promised myself I'd finally learn to surf. Man, I really needed this vacation.

Big shot Brad had already announced that this would be his last family vacation. He thinks he's getting too old to go away with Mom and Dad. If I had the money, I'd send him on his own vacation—to Pluto.

Dad came home from work later than usual that night, and when I walked into the kitchen, I knew something was up. Mom and Dad were talking in those low voices they use when they're fighting or if there's something unexpected, like a $2,000 plumbing bill.

"Anything wrong?" I asked.

"No, Andy. Of course not," said Mom. But she never was a very good liar.

They called Brad in for dinner a third time, and he finally sat down at the table. Dad always insists that we eat together when he's home. As we passed around the dishes, Dad asked us about our day. Mom told some lame story about the supermarket and meeting the baby-sitter we had when I was, like, two. This story, not surprisingly, was met with dead silence.

"You want to hear something *really* funny?" I asked. Then I told them about my brilliant new defense during our little basketball game. Dad laughed so hard he almost choked on his meat loaf. But Mom didn't see the humor in it.

"You actually pulled your pants down in our driveway?" she asked, appalled. "What will our neighbors think?" The look on her face made me, Brad, and Dad laugh even harder.

Then Dad asked Brad what was new with him. He gave his standard answer, "Nothing," then asked Dad to pass the peas.

Seeing how that pissed Dad off, I tried to lighten things up.

"Actually, Brad had a big day. He got himself a new comb."

"Yeah," Brad shot back, "and I'm going to shove it up your—"

"Bradley!" Mom said, as if she'd never heard this kind of talk before. Just another typical dinner at Casa Crenshaw.

Finally, it was Dad's turn. "I've got some good news, guys! I've just been promoted to West Coast vice president!"

"Whoa! Alright, Dad!" I shouted. Brad woke up and congratulated him, too. But I could tell something wasn't quite right. Mom obviously already knew about the promotion, and as happy as she tried to look, I knew there was more to this story. Dad worked for one of the biggest paper companies in the country, and he'd always done a lot of traveling. He told us he'd be doing even more now.

"They're sending me to Seattle and Portland, and then I have to go to a company retreat in Denver. I'm leaving here on Saturday, so we're going to have to postpone the trip to Hawaii for a while."

This couldn't be happening. I yelled the first thing that came to my mind: "Dad, you can't do this to me!" But I knew it was good-bye, Hawaii. I'd have a better chance of getting there now if I swam.

"Guys, we're really sorry, but this has just come up. And it's a big, important step in Dad's career."

"We'll try to work in a vacation later this summer," Dad said, but I could tell even *he* didn't believe it.

"Yeah, right," I said, staring down at my plate. I felt like this giant beach ball, and someone had let all the air out. I started crushing the peas on my plate with my fork, trying to kill every last one of them. One shot across the table and hit Brad in the neck. He got that look in his eye and kicked me hard under the table.

Then, without any warning, the news went from bad to even worse: "Your mother's coming with me on this trip," Dad announced.

"Wives of vice presidents get to come along," she told us, with a smile.

This got Brad's full attention. "No big deal, I'll just stay here and baby-sit the kid." Man, was he ever clueless!

"Sorry, Brad, but I don't think anyone's ready for that," Mom said. "We've made arrangements for you boys to go stay with Aunt Karen and Uncle Jim."

"What?" I protested. "We hardly even know them!"

Brad was a little more articulate. "Screw that! There's no way I'm getting shipped off to some farm in Wisconsin with some wacko uncle and aunt. I'm not going anywhere!"

"That's a terrible thing to say," Dad said. "Jim's your uncle and Karen's his wife, so have a little respect!" As he said this, that vein in his forehead started to bulge.

Brad leaped out of his chair, slammed the table, and stormed out of the kitchen. I'd never seen him so mad.

So now it was up to me, the younger brother, to be the mature one. But I didn't want to be the mature one. I wanted to go to Hawaii! Mom came toward me with a hug in mind, but I knew that if she put her arms around me, I'd lose it completely. I got up, slipped past her, and escaped out the back door. Then I headed straight for my hideaway.

✥

At the farthest corner of the backyard, behind an overgrown pine tree, there are two loose boards in the redwood fence. You can crawl under on your stomach to get to the other side. There's a 10-foot space between our fence and the one behind us; it's cramped and covered with weeds, but it's my own little corner of the world.

I discovered this spot by accident when I was looking for a lost baseball. I still keep that baseball there, along with some books, water, candy bars, and an old handheld video game. I store them in an old crate I keep hidden with rocks, leaves, and sticks.

I go there when I need to think or when things really get bad. I went there the night before I had hernia surgery, and I memorized all my lines there the night before I starred in the school play. I went there when I dropped the fly ball that lost us a playoff game. This spot had seen me through some tough times, and that night was no exception.

I took my iPod out of my pocket and cranked up the first song. I made it loud enough to drown out the world, then picked up the old baseball and started throwing it against the fence. How could this be happening? I threw the ball a bit harder. Here I was, two days from a great vacation, and now instead I was going to be stuck on some smelly farm in Wisconsin with my brother—who happens to hate my guts. I threw that ball even harder. It didn't take me long to put a hole in that fence.

4
Godzilla

If you ever want a true definition of chaos, forget looking in the dictionary. Just watch my family getting ready to go to the airport.

We were supposed to leave at 9:00 a.m. It was 8:14, and Brad wasn't even up yet. Dad was still in his underwear, and he was wearing only one sock. A maniac, he was bouncing around the house with a clipboard in one hand and a cup of coffee in the other, calling out last-minute instructions to everyone.

"Lock the windows, set the light timers, and leave a note for the gardener. Brad, get your butt out of bed—now! Emily, where's my other sock?"

Mom came into the living room wheeling two bulging suitcases. "Everything's taken care of, Martin. I stopped the newspaper, Mrs. Bergin's picking up the mail, and your other sock's in the cat's litter box."

Dad looked a little nauseous. "That's the third pair of socks this week. The cat has a serious sock fetish, and he's a kleptomaniac. He needs professional help."

Mom cut in, "I think we'll have a lot less trouble with airport security if you put your pants on."

"But I'm *trying* to get dressed," Dad protested.

Brad came down the stairs, rubbing his eyes, still half asleep. "Nice look, Dad," he commented.

"Don't worry about me, buster. You've got 44 minutes to get yourself packed, or we're going to leave you here."

"Works for me," Brad said, with a smirk.

"Don't start that again," Dad warned.

In the last couple of days, they'd given us these pep talks. We even had a family meeting, and their words were always the same: "Be mature about this." "Keep an open mind." "Think of it as a new experience." And then there was my personal favorite: "Sometimes in life, you have to do things you don't want to do." You get the general idea.

9:53 a.m. We were in the driveway, the bags packed, the car running, and of course, we were late. Dad was sweating and cursing under his breath. Mom was blaming Dad, Dad was blaming Brad, Brad was actually blaming the cat, and I had my own problems. Because I'm the shortest, I was stuck with the three carry-on bags under my feet. My knees were all the way up under my chin, and there was another suitcase between me and Brad that was digging into my ribs. By the time we got to the airport, they'd be able to store *me* in the overhead bin with the carry-on bags.

We pulled out of the driveway and headed down the street.

"The tickets!" Mom shouted.

Dad slammed on the brakes, and everyone flew forward. Everyone except me, of course. I was wedged in for life. Mom ran out to get the plane tickets as Dad gripped the steering wheel even tighter.

Mom hurried back to the car, and Dad pulled out to the street. We almost made it to the corner this time.

"My pills!" Mom cried.

"I don't believe this!" Dad barked. "Get your damn pills, and while you're at it, get something strong for me."

Brad and I started laughing. What else could we do? Then Mom came back to the car, out of breath and sweating. Unlike Brad, she never sweats—unless we're late for the airport.

"Now, do we have everything, everybody?" Dad asked through clenched teeth. "Can we leave now, please?"

Once again, we headed for the airport. Brad waited until we were two blocks from home, then said, "I've got to pee."

"You're the reason we're late in the first place!" Dad yelled. "You don't deserve to pee."

"Ever again?" Brad asked.

This time, we all cracked up. I even saw a little smile from Dad in the rearview mirror.

⁙

Dad fought his way through traffic, and we pulled into the airport parking lot at 10:50 a.m. It took two people to pry me out of the car.

Mom and Dad were leaving first, on an 11:30 a.m. flight to Seattle. Brad and I were flying out two hours later. The plan was for Mom and Dad to drop us at our gate and then go catch their plane. We were taking a nonstop to Chicago, then getting on a smaller plane to Madison. Aunt

Karen and Uncle Jim would pick us up and take us to their house near Oshkosh.

I love airports and always have. There aren't many places more alive than an airport. You can actually feel the energy there.

On the way to the gate, we passed thousands of people, everyone in a hurry. I wondered where they could all be going and where they were all coming from. I wished I could trade tickets with just about any one of them, since practically any place else would be better than Wisconsin.

We arrived at Gate 62, and Mom watched as we checked in. Then Dad nervously pointed to his watch. "Honey, we've got to go right now if we want to make our flight."

Thankfully, there was no time left for sentiment, no time for them to get all mushy on us. Instead, we got a 10-minute good-bye compressed into 60 seconds:

Mom: Promise me you'll be careful.
Dad: Keep an open mind, guys.
Mom: Don't forget to use sunscreen.
Dad: Think of this as an adventure.
Mom: And please change your underwear every day.
Dad: Remember, you're guests, so behave like it.
Mom: I love you! I'll miss you!
Dad: Have fun, guys.
Mom: We'll call you tonight.

Hugs all around, and then they were gone. Brad and I found the last two empty seats and sat down with our carry-on bags. Mom had packed us lunch, dinner, a first-aid kit, and a family photo. She really was some piece of work.

"So, what do you want to do for the next two hours?" I asked my brother.

"I'm going to check out the newsstand. Stay here and watch our stuff." Before I could protest, Brad took off and I was stuck with the bags. I guess there's a metaphor for my life in there somewhere. So there I sat for an hour and 45 minutes, afraid to leave our stuff. To kill some time, I read my ESPN magazine and listened to my iPod. When I got really bored, I picked out people in the gate area and made up whole stories about where they were going and why. You'd be amazed at how many turned out to be spies.

Finally, just as we were called to board our flight, Brad casually walked over.

"Thanks a lot, dickwad," I said.

"Hey, what's the big deal? I'll watch the bags on the flight home."

Man, he can be such a pain in the butt sometimes.

My brother and I were no longer speaking as we boarded the plane. We walked down the aisle to Row 27, where we had the middle and window seats. Brad quickly put the bags into the overhead compartment, then took the window seat. I sat down next to him, in the dreaded center seat.

"I get the window on the way back," I warned. Brad just sat there and stared at the seatback in front of him, as if I didn't exist. Man, was he ever pissed off about this rotten trip. I guess the reality of where we actually were going had finally hit him full force. But I couldn't just sit there like this, and I had to say something to him.

"Look, Brad, I don't like this any more than you do,

but since we're in this together, let's at least try to get along. Okay?"

Dead silence. Brad was now staring out the window. Then, a full two minutes later, he spoke.

"You're right, we are in this together." He put out his hand, and I slapped him five. He does have his moments, even if they do come once every six months. But now that he was talking again, I started feeling better. I knew I really needed him on this trip, and maybe this time he'd actually be there for me for a change. I looked down the aisle and watched a pretty flight attendant as she loaded drinks onto a cart. And that's when I saw HIM.

He was only about five foot three, but he was wide and obese—probably at least 400 pounds. He had to walk down the aisle sideways. Even then, his massive gut and enormous butt scraped against anyone sitting on either side of the aisle.

As he got closer to our row, I said a silent prayer: "Please don't sit next to me. Please, God, don't let him sit next to me."

I just couldn't look. As he approached our row, I closed my eyes, and when I opened them, he was gone. But just as I breathed a big sigh of relief, he was back, standing by my row.

"Here it is, 27-D," he said.

I watched in horror as the fattest man in North America wedged himself into the seat beside me. Because I never wanted to know his name, I decided to call him Godzilla. He smiled, trying to be friendly, and I forced a smile back. His shirt looked like a circus tent with a collar, and I tried hard not to stare.

29

Godzilla took the armrest between us and shoved it into the upright position to give himself more room. Then he slid toward me, now taking up his seat and half of mine. His thighs, stomach, and arms were all squashed against me. We were like this freaky set of unmatched Siamese twins, and I was coming down with a serious case of claustrophobia.

I turned to Brad—big mistake. He had his hand over his mouth, trying to stifle a laugh.

"This is *so* not funny," I whispered. Then Brad totally lost it. He put his head in the air sickness bag and turned to face the window. I could see his shoulders shaking.

I slid away from Godzilla as far as I possibly could, but the blob of flesh on my left just followed me as I moved. How would I last four hours to Chicago? I picked up the emergency exit card from the seat pocket in front of me and memorized all the exits. I so wanted to get to one of them in a hurry, away from this whale of a seatmate.

By now, we were in the air, and the flight attendant came by, taking drink orders from Godzilla and Brad. As she started moving up the aisle, I called out, "What about me?"

"I'm sorry," she said, "I never even saw you there."

No kidding. Godzilla ordered two double scotches. He devoured his bag of honey-roasted peanuts and then began eyeing mine. By now, I'd lost my appetite, possibly forever, and drummed my fingers nervously on the tray table.

"Mind if I eat those?" he asked, practically drooling.

For a second I panicked, afraid he meant my fingers. I

quickly handed over my peanuts, then he patted my head with his fat paw.

I told myself that I could do this, I'd just have to hang in there for a few hours. Then, without warning, my worst nightmare came true. Godzilla fell asleep. His head fell to the side, and naturally, it had to be my side. Next came his shoulders and then the biggest stomach I'd ever seen. Before I knew what was happening, the massive passenger was fast asleep—on me. I now was completely pinned by a human avalanche—and it was snoring and smelled like scotch.

Brad finally noticed my predicament, and now even he looked worried. He tried to pull me out, but he couldn't do it alone. Godzilla had passed out cold and was what you could call dead weight.

The pilot got on the intercom. "Folks, you're in for a rare treat. Normally, we don't fly this route, but because of thunderstorms, we're flying over the Grand Canyon, one of the Seven Natural Wonders of the World."

Big deal. I was being smothered by the *eighth*.

Brad frantically waved for the flight attendant. She took one look at me and gasped, "Oh, no. You poor kid!"

Then, for the next 10 minutes, Brad, two flight attendants, and a fireman from Long Beach all pulled and tugged, trying to free me from my trap. Working like a tug-of-war team, they maximized their leverage and finally pulled me out.

By now, the entire plane was cheering. I was a bit shaken and smelled like scotch, but otherwise I was okay. The flight attendants felt so bad about what had happened that they moved Brad and me to empty seats in first class. When the plane landed, I got to meet the pilot, who said I was a very brave guy.

First class is awesome. The food's actually edible, the seats are really comfortable, and you have your own movie screen.

"This is sweet," Brad said, stretching out his legs. "Let's make sure you get trapped under somebody on the flight home, too."

I hit him in the face with my first-class pillow and fell asleep somewhere over Kansas.

5
Cheese and Other Smelly Things

"Ladies and gentlemen, we'll be landing in about 12 minutes, so please fasten your seat belts, return your seats to the upright position, and secure all tray tables."

As we descended, the change in cabin pressure made my ears hurt big time. Brad and I changed planes in Chicago, boarding a smaller, noisier plane. Then, after more than eight hours in airplanes and airports, we were finally about to land in Madison, Wisconsin.

My heart started beating faster as I thought about Aunt Karen and Uncle Jim. I hardly knew these people. We'd seen them a few times when I was really young and one other time at a family reunion in San Diego a while back. But that had been, like, six years ago, and to me, these people were really still strangers.

According to Mom, Uncle Jim, her older brother, is the "sweetest guy in the world." The way she tells it, he had everything going for him: he was the star pitcher on his high school baseball team, and he was even drafted by the Houston Astros. But he was also drafted by the U.S. Army right around the same time.

Uncle Jim went to Vietnam, and right before he was supposed to come home, he got shot in the shoulder. The doctors told him he'd never again throw a baseball, and Mom said it changed him forever.

After he recovered, Uncle Jim went to college for a while, but then he finally dropped out, and I mean he really dropped out. He became a hippie and, for a long time, lived in a van. He met Aunt Karen at a commune, a place where Dad says everyone eats together, sleeps together, and runs around naked. Sounds like fun to me.

Uncle Jim and Aunt Karen drove around the country for years, working all kinds of interesting jobs. They taught on an Indian reservation, fished for tuna, worked the oil fields in Alaska, and were actors in a traveling theatre group.

They finally settled down on a small farm in Wisconsin, along with a few goats and some chickens and pigs. But they don't really farm very much. Mom says Uncle Jim gets bored easily and is always trying out new jobs and careers. Last I heard, he was a part-time DJ on the local FM radio station. For years, they'd invited us to come visit, but we never managed to go. I guess that made Brad and me the guinea pigs.

As the plane banked left and headed for the runway, I looked over at Brad. He was chewing on a fingernail.

"You ready?" I asked.

"Like I've got a choice here?"

"Maybe it won't be that bad."

"Dude, it's gonna be a disaster." Leave it to my brother to look on the bright side.

✳

We stepped off the plane into the cool evening air. It was a lot different from the heavy, foggy air of San Francisco. The small terminal was more like a bus station, but it featured an oversized sign: WELCOME TO WISCONSIN: THE BIG CHEESE!

Brad took one look and grumbled, "I hate cheese." We were off to a great start.

I looked around for a couple that could be them. Then I heard the scream. When I turned, I saw this woman wearing bright pink pants and a Grateful Dead T-shirt. And she was running at me full speed. Everyone in the room stopped to watch as Aunt Karen sped toward me like a torpedo.

She was plump, with a mass of frizzy hair in several shades of red. As she ran, she jiggled all over, but she looked relatively harmless—except for this half-crazed smile. I braced myself.

"Here they are, and they're all grown up! You must be Andy!"

Before I could answer, she wrestled me into a bear hug and lifted me right off the ground.

"That's me," I grunted, trying to get my wind back and hoping my ribs were just bruised instead of fractured.

"And getta load of this one," Aunt Karen announced, looking up at Brad. "He's huge. You're all grown up, aren't you, Bradley!"

Aunt Karen hugged Brad, who hugged her back with one arm. He definitely wasn't as thrilled.

"Nice to see you again, too, he replied. And it's *Brad*."

"He's got an attitude. I like that!" Aunt Karen smacked Brad playfully, then let out this amazing laugh. It was a deep, cackling, scary laugh that filled the entire terminal.

"Don't mind her. Karen was abandoned by her parents and raised by hyenas," said the man who was following behind her.

This had to be Uncle Jim. He was tall and thin, with long grey hair reaching almost to his shoulders. He wore a denim jacket over a black T-shirt and had a hoop earring in one ear. Uncle Jim seemed very laid back and looked pretty cool for an old guy.

"It's great to see you boys. How were your flights?" Uncle Jim asked.

"Fine," Brad answered.

"Easy for you to say," I said. "I was almost crushed to death by a 400-pound man."

Aunt Karen must've thought I was kidding, because she let loose with that crazy laugh again.

"He's got some imagination, doesn't he, Jim?"

"Let me take your bags, guys. We sure have some catching up to do," Uncle Jim said.

Then Aunt Karen opened a shopping bag and shoved a huge wheel of cheese into Brad's arms.

"Welcome to Wisconsin, guys!"

"What's this?" Brad asked, stunned.

"It's 14 pounds of real Wisconsin cheddar. And it's all for you. Oh, we're going to have SO MUCH FUN!"

Aunt Karen grabbed Brad and me into a three-way hug, pressing Brad's nose against the real Wisconsin cheddar.

"Just kill me now," he muttered.

As we drove away from the airport, Aunt Karen was talking a mile a minute, wanting to know everything about our lives. Since Brad wasn't exactly bubbling over with enthusiasm, I got stuck filling them in about school, Mom and Dad, our activities, the usual. Whenever I said something even remotely funny, Aunt Karen cackled until the car windows shook. I noticed the more she laughed, the lower Brad sank in his seat.

Aunt Karen kept exclaiming, "I can't believe how you two've grown," until Uncle Jim finally had had enough of it.

"Karen, it's been six years since we saw these guys. That's what teenagers do—they grow."

"I guess you're right," she admitted. "Forgive me, you guys. I'm just not so used to being with kids. Jim and I can't have children—he has an abnormally low sperm count."

With that, Uncle Jim swerved the car.

"How 'bout those Packers," Brad blurted out, trying desperately to change the subject.

"Karen," Uncle Jim said, "that's not part of the tour. Why on earth would you tell them something like that?"

"Oh, lighten up, Jimmy, they're family!"

"Hey, why don't we just tell everybody else?"

Then, possibly to break the tension or maybe because he was also just plain nuts like our aunt, Uncle Jim rolled down his window and shouted to a trucker next to him, "Hey, I'm sterile. I'm reproductively challenged!" Then, passing a car with an open window: "I can't have kids!"

The driver stared at Uncle Jim, shook his head, and sped away. I glanced over at Brad, who had this look on his face that pleaded, "Somebody get me out of here!"

"All right, Jim, I think you've made your point."

"Sorry, guys," he apologized. "We're not usually this crazy."

"Speak for yourself, Jim," said our aunt. Then she turned to Brad and asked, "Are we having fun yet?"

"Well, looks like one of us is," Brad shot back.

"I see this one's gonna take some work," she announced.

As we drove farther away from Madison, the towns got smaller and farther apart. We passed lots of farms and heard the mooing of many cows. Aunt Karen and Uncle Jim lived on the outskirts of Oshkosh. Before we knew it, we drove up a long dirt road that led to a small farmhouse, and Uncle Jim parked the truck.

"This is it, guys."

Stepping out of the car, I was hit by the strong odor of animal droppings. A stable where a few horses grazed was on one side of the house. Then I was startled by a loud snorting noise.

"It's okay," Uncle Jim laughed, seeing me jump. "That's just one of the pigs."

"Margaret!" Aunt Karen scolded the pig. "These are very special guests. Now, you mind your manners."

The pig stopped snorting instantly. It was actually kind of weird—she seemed to understand my crazy aunt.

"Watch where you step, boys, this isn't San Francisco," Aunt Karen warned.

"No kidding," Brad said, obviously not too impressed.

The minute we stepped into the house, a huge hairy dog bounded across the living room and jumped right up on me. We were eye to eye as he stood there, panting in my face with that hot breath of his.

"That's Clyde," Jim said, "the laziest dog on the planet."

Clyde whimpered, and Aunt Karen looked sternly at Uncle Jim.

"Jim, you've hurt his feelings again."

"Yeah, like dogs have feelings," Brad scoffed.

"They do, Bradley. And you're not helping."

"Karen thinks she has this ESP thing with animals," Uncle Jim said.

"I do. Just ask Clyde," Aunt Karen said, dead serious.

Uncle Jim wisely changed the subject. "You guys must be starving," he said. He guided us into the kitchen and turned on the overhead light. There on the kitchen table was the biggest stash of junk food I'd ever seen in my life. They had boxes of cookies, all kinds of chips and pretzels, plus cupcakes, candy bars, licorice, and more. It would take a month to finish it all.

"Whoa! You guys know how to eat," I said, approving.

"I didn't know exactly what teenage boys like, so I just bought three of everything," Aunt Karen said, proudly.

"Thanks," I said, "but Mom doesn't let us eat much of this kind of stuff."

"Well, she's not here, and you're on vacation, so why not live a little?"

I shrugged and tore into a bag.

"That's the spirit," Aunt Karen said. "Get him a glass of milk, Jim. What about you, Bradley? I mean, *Brad*."

"No, thanks, I'm not really hungry. I think I'll just fire up my laptop and talk to some friends online."

Aunt Karen frowned. "Sorry, but that's not going to be possible."

"You guys don't have the Internet?" Brad asked.

"We do. I mean, we did. But last week, Sylvester, one of our pigs, ate right through the cable."

"It's the same cable for our TV, so right now they're both out," Uncle Jim said.

"So you have no Internet *and* no TV?" I asked, trying to digest the unimaginable: two weeks stuck in the boonies with no e-mail, Facebook, MTV, or ESPN. Great. It was even worse than I thought.

Brad, meanwhile, was starting to lose it. I could tell because his nostrils were flaring. He looked around the room like a trapped animal, then asked, "So what are you going to do about it?"

"Don't worry," Aunt Karen said, "I've already done it. I scolded Sylvester and sent him to bed without his dinner."

"I mean what are you going to do about the *cable*?" Brad asked in a shaky, raised voice.

"Oh, we're getting it fixed," Uncle Jim said. "But the cable folks won't be back this way again for at least another month."

"Don't look so glum, boys," Aunt Karen said. "You can survive for a week without going online. It's just the Internet, not a heart-lung machine."

"There're plenty of other things to do here," she continued. "When was the last time you took a walk outside in the fresh air? Or rode a horse? Or really tried to talk to a pig?"

Man, were we in trouble.

6

O Brother, Where Art Thou?

It was late, even by West Coast time, but neither of us could sleep. I sat up in bed, watching Brad pace around the guest room. He was pissed—so pissed that his voice was cracking. I thought he was going to lose it.

"We've got to get the hell out of here, Andy."

"Come on, Brad, get real."

"I'm serious. There's no way I'm going to last two whole weeks here."

Brad was losing it, alright. This meant I had to be the mature brother again. I hate it when that happens.

"We just got here," I said. "Just try and give it a chance."

"Give what a chance? This place is in the middle of nowhere, there's no Internet or TV, and nothing around for miles. What are we going to do for a week besides step in horse crap?"

Since I had already stepped in some, I wasn't quite sure how to answer him. But I had to think of something. "I don't know, but I'm sure there's some kind of town around here and there's got to be *something* to do there."

"Face it, Andy, we're stuck in hell. They just happen to call it Wisconsin."

"Brad, you're such a downer sometimes. You need a better attitude."

"You sound just like Dad."

He was right, but I wasn't trying to.

"Another thing," Brad continued. "These people might be family, but they're crazy."

"Okay, they are a little different," I admitted.

"Uncle Jim's different. Aunt Karen's *nuts*. The lady talks to animals. She already doesn't like me, and even the dog's giving me strange looks."

"You're getting paranoid, Brad. You haven't exactly been Mr. Sunshine, you know."

"It's not about me, man! It's about being bored out of our skulls."

I really didn't know what to say. Then, Brad got that look in his eye. It was the same look he had had when he tried to shave our cat with Dad's electric shaver.

"Look, I've got a plan. We've got plane tickets, and we've got money, right? I say we leave them a nice note. Then we sneak out and hitchhike into town, catch a bus to the airport, and go home."

Did I mention that Brad wasn't very bright?

"Brad, that's the dumbest thing you've ever said."

This was saying a lot, since it was Brad who had once said George Washington fought in the Industrial Revolution.

I tried to reason with him. "We can't just get up and leave. Then we'd be, like, runaways. Our faces would end up on an Amber Alert!"

"Jeez, Andy, you've got no sense of adventure."

"Well, you've got no sense at all!"

"Thank you, Dad!"

"I don't care if I sound like Dad. You're talking crazy, and we're not going anywhere. We just got here. At least give it a couple of days."

Just then my cell rang. Mom was calling to check in on us. The ultimate optimist, I told her we were fine and everything was cool. She bought it, right up until Brad shouted at the top of his lungs, "Get me out of here!" I assured her that Brad was kidding and she hung up quickly, not wanting any part of this.

Brad threw a pillow against the wall and fell into bed. End of discussion. I sat there in silence, not knowing what to think. What if he was right about this place? There didn't seem to be much to do, and Aunt Karen was a little strange. I had no idea what we were in for.

✢

I was having that dream again—the one about the *Sports Illustrated* swimsuit cover girl . . . you know, the one in the lime green string bikini. We're on a beach in Fiji, and I'm the famous swimsuit issue photographer. She's posing for me and looking very hot. She's also a little sweaty, which makes her look even hotter.

I say, "Great work, babe. Let's take a break." She climbs off the rock she was posing on and walks seductively toward me. She leads me into the makeup tent. She puts her arms around my waist. Our bodies are touching.

We look into each other's eyes, and we kiss. It's a serious wet kiss.

Then I woke up to find Clyde, the big hairy dog, licking my face like it was a pork chop. His hot, smelly breath brought me to my senses. This ain't Fiji, and Clyde's no supermodel.

I checked my watch, which was still on San Francisco time. It was 6:15 a.m., and 8:15 a.m. in Wisconsin. Brad's bed was empty, which was odd because he never gets up early. Maybe he woke up to pee. I sat up and blinked the sleep from my eyes. Then I saw the note. It was taped to my suitcase, where I couldn't miss it. I jumped out of bed and, with my hands shaking, unfolded the paper and saw Brad's handwriting.

Andy: If you don't know by now, I split. I just had to get out of here. I know you think I'm all talk and no action, but maybe this'll show you I'm not. You had the chance to come with me, but I understand that you're scared. I left your airline ticket and some money, but I took most of it, 'cause I'll need it more. Hope you're not too bored. Love you, bro.

Great. My genius brother had actually run away. I couldn't believe it! Brad *was* all talk and no action. He'd always make these grand plans, but he never followed through with any of them. So now, 2,000 miles from home, in the middle of nowhere, he had finally grown a pair and decided to go for it—and leave me behind, alone with two virtual strangers.

What can I say? My brother is an idiot. But as mad as I was and as stupid as I knew he was, Brad was still my brother and I immediately started to worry about him.

45

I had this vision of him hitchhiking, then getting picked up by an axe murderer. The guy drives him all the way to Alaska, but dummy Brad just thinks we're having a record-cold early winter and that he's actually on his way home. The axe murderer would be really nice, buy him a burger with everything on it, talk to him about baseball, then chop him into a zillion pieces and bury him where we'd never find him. Totally convinced by then that this was going to happen, I went into automatic crisis mode: I got nauseous.

I ran full speed out of the bedroom and plowed smack into Aunt Karen, who was wrapped in a towel and soaking wet from her shower. I guess I startled her, because she screamed. Then I screamed, too. I mean, just looking at her was scary: a huge pile of dripping wet red hair, pasty white skin, and, where the towel had slipped, a lot more of my aunt than I'd ever wanted to see. I'd waited 15 years to see live breasts, and believe me, this was not how I'd imagined them.

"Where's the fire, kid?"

"Brad was chopped up by an axe murderer!" That didn't exactly come out right, so I rephrased it. "Brad's gone!"

"What do you mean, gone?"

"*Gone* gone. He ran away," I said.

"Damn. Does he do this often?"

"This is the first time."

"And he's gotta do it on my watch. I've never even had a pig run away."

"I know, but pigs are smart. We really have to do something now!" I insisted.

"You're right, but there's no need to panic," she said. Then she desperately screamed, "Jim!"

Uncle Jim must've known what that scream meant—he was inside a few seconds later.

"The big one's run away," Aunt Karen said.

"Hmm. I didn't think you were calling me in to breakfast," Jim said, way too calmly.

Well, someone sure had to panic at this point, so I stepped right up. "Guys, my brother is missing! Are you just going to stand there, or what?"

"Don't worry, he won't get far," Uncle Jim said. "I'll get on the horn and tell Sheriff Stucky to make some calls and look around. Meanwhile, we'll go looking for him."

A few minutes later, we all were in the pickup truck. Uncle Jim drove while Aunt Karen called the locals and I scoured the roads with binoculars.

I told them about Brad's birdbrained plan to get back to Madison and fly home. Aunt Karen called the bus station, where Brad would have to go to get back to the airport. Unless, of course, he hitched a ride from someone. Like, possibly . . . an axe murderer.

We pulled up to the bus station, and Uncle Jim and I went inside. The station was empty, except for an old man sleeping in a chair and a lady watching a coin-operated TV. It was a creepy place, dark and depressing. Uncle Jim went up to the ticket agent behind the counter. He described Brad and was told no one like that had come in. Then he gave the agent his cell-phone number and asked him to call if Brad showed up.

When we got back to the truck, Aunt Karen was waiting with a huge grin.

"Just got a call from Sheriff Stucky. He said Tommy Pierce was driving his mail truck on the highway and saw a kid hitchhiking with a suitcase. Sheriff wanted to pick him up, but I told him we'd rather go get him ourselves."

"Good thinking," Uncle Jim said. "No need to scare the kid. But I do think it's a good time for a little lesson." He and Aunt Karen smiled at each other while I wondered what was so damn amusing.

It turns out that Uncle Jim has a wicked sense of humor, as I was about to find out. Instead of driving straight to rescue Brad, we instead went to the nearest truck stop, which was bustling with big rigs, oil tankers, and dairy trucks, all crisscrossing the country to get their cargo to market.

But Uncle Jim was interested in a specific kind of cargo. He drove around until he spotted a truck full of chickens. Inside the cab, eating a sandwich, was a rugged-looking man. Uncle Jim said he was Ned Thatcher. We waited in the pickup while Uncle Jim spoke to Ned, and soon they both were laughing. Then Ned got out of the truck and handed Uncle Jim the keys.

Soon I was sitting in the cab of the chicken truck, along with Uncle Jim. Through the sliding glass window behind us, I could see 800 chickens in the cargo bed, clucking like crazy, with feathers flying everywhere.

As we sped down the highway, Uncle Jim let me in on his little joke. This was going to be good!

Sure enough, Brad was a quarter of a mile ahead, sitting on his suitcase by the side of the two-lane highway. As we approached, Uncle Jim told me to crouch down on the floor and keep as quiet as I could. He then slipped on a big cowboy hat and pulled his collar up to conceal most of his face. As I scrunched down, I felt the truck slow to a stop.

"Where you headed, son?" said Uncle Jim, disguising his voice.

"I'm trying to get back to Madison. I want to go to the airport," I heard Brad say through the partially open window.

"Well, you're in luck, kid. I'm going in that direction," Uncle Jim said.

"That's great. Thanks a lot, mister," Brad said.

"But you can't ride up here. I've got tuberculosis, and it's very contagious, and I can't expose you to these germs." I started to laugh, and Uncle Jim nudged me with his boot. "Climb in back, kid. Don't worry, those chickens are friendly."

Brad uttered one of his typical frustrated sighs. Then I could hear him climbing up the side of the truck, followed by a loud thud. He'd thrown in his suitcase, sending the chickens into a frenzy. Next, I heard Brad jump into the truck, followed by the screeching and cackling of 800 angry chickens.

"Ah, ow, get away from me, bird!" Brad yelled. "Stop pecking me! Shoo! Shoo! Hey, mister, they're all pecking me."

By now, Uncle Jim and I were laughing, and he opened the sliding window behind us.

"Just get over here by the window and stand still. Then they'll let you be."

With that, Uncle Jim stomped on the gas pedal and the truck lurched forward, throwing Brad off balance and knocking him onto the truck's disgusting floor.

"Dammit!" he screamed. "I just fell in a bunch of chicken shit!"

By now I was laughing so hard I actually started to snort.

"Well, yeah," Uncle Jim said. "I can't exactly take 800 chickens into a restroom at the Holiday Inn, can I?"

"Guess not," Brad muttered, backing off a bit.

"So, where you coming from, kid?"

"My parents dumped me with my aunt and uncle on some farm near Oshkosh. But there's no way I can stay at that crazy place."

"Oshkosh? That wouldn't be the Clooney farm, would it?"

"Yeah. You know them?" Brad asked.

"Heard about 'em. Word is those folks are nuts."

"Tell me about it," Brad said.

"They're known around here as the Looney Clooneys."

"No kidding," Brad said. "Even their dog's kinda weird."

"And I heard the guy, what's his name?"

"Jim."

"I heard he eats cat food and keeps mice in his pocket."

"Whoa," Brad said, "that's way worse than I thought."

My stomach was now aching as I tried to hold my breath to keep from laughing. Uncle Jim was really good at this charade. He really had Brad going.

We pulled off the highway and started driving the back roads. A nervous Brad approached the window.

"Excuse me, mister, but are you sure this is the way to the Madison airport?"

"You bet," Uncle Jim assured him as he winked down at me. "This is the shortcut. We won't have to hit all that traffic."

That was a good one, since there were, like, two cars on the road. I'm sure Brad was getting suspicious, but really, what could he do? He was just another chicken stuck back there with the rest of them.

Before long, we pulled into the driveway back at Uncle Jim and Aunt Karen's place.

Brad began raising his voice now, getting really agitated. "Why are we stopping here? What do you think you're doing, mister?"

Uncle Jim took off the cowboy hat and jumped out of the truck, and I quickly followed to a spot where Brad could now see us both.

"Welcome home, Brad," Uncle Jim said, smiling.

"Hey, bro," I added casually.

From the back of the truck, Brad let out this wounded animal scream, then started kicking the side of the truck in frustration. But this only made the chickens angrier, and they started to back him against the wall. By now, Uncle Jim and I were laughing so hard that we leaned on the truck to stay upright.

"This is so not funny! Not one tiny bit!" Brad screamed.

"Are you kidding, bro? This is *hilarious*," I said.

Brad picked up his suitcase, raised it over his head, and threw it at me from the back of the truck. I sidestepped it easily as it hit the ground and burst open, spilling Brad's clothes all over and smearing them with dirt. He climbed out of the truck and jumped down, his pants all covered with chicken shit. He truly looked pathetic.

Embarrassed and exhausted, he sat down on a rock, putting his head in his hands.

I didn't know what to do. It was one of the few times in my life that I actually felt sorry for my brother. I walked over and put my hand on his shoulder. He didn't look up, but at least he didn't knock my hand away. Then Uncle Jim came over.

"You got me. I'm humiliated, okay? Are you happy now?" Brad blurted out.

"Look, Brad, we were just having a little fun with you. It's better we picked you up than some homicidal maniac. The thing is, hitchhiking is dangerous, Brad. It wasn't a smart thing to do."

"I know," Brad said.

"Tell me," Uncle Jim said, "are we really so weird that you had to just get up and run?"

Finally, Brad looked up. "I don't know. I just felt so trapped, stuck out here in the middle of nowhere. No offense, but, like, what the hell is there to do out here, anyway?"

Uncle Jim chuckled.

"It's a fair question," I said.

"Yes, it is," Uncle Jim replied. "Look, fellas, this may not be a big city, but it's not Siberia either. There's more to this little town than you think. Trust me. I've got a few things up my sleeve."

That's when we heard the screeching of tires. We looked up to see Aunt Karen skidding the pickup through the gate, stopping short in a cloud of dust. She bounced out of the truck and made a beeline straight toward Brad.

"Bradley Crenshaw, have you lost *all* your marbles? Give me one good reason I shouldn't get on the phone right now and call your mother."

Brad looked at her hopefully. "Because you're way too cool for that?"

Aunt Karen thought about this for a second, then nodded. "True. Okay, what do you boys want for breakfast?"

Brad smiled for the first time since we'd gotten there. He must have been thinking the same thing I was: maybe there's hope for these people yet.

7
The Taste of Mud

When Uncle Jim said he had a few things up his sleeve, he wasn't kidding. After an enormous Midwestern breakfast of pancakes, bacon, grits, and homemade bread, I could hardly move.

"Time to get moving, fellas," Uncle Jim announced.

"Moving where?" Brad asked.

"You guys like baseball?"

❖

Twenty minutes later, we were in the front seat of the pickup with the window down and the cool morning air pleasantly blowing on our faces. We were heading down Highway 41 toward Oshkosh, to a date with the Oshkosh Cubs.

The Oshkosh Cubs were the single-A minor league team owned by the real Chicago Cubs. Uncle Jim turned out to actually have a whole bunch of different jobs. He was a part-time DJ at the local FM radio station, he was a part-time massage therapist, and lucky for us, he was also the part-time trainer for the Oshkosh Cubs. To our amazement, he'd arranged for us to work out on the field with real professional baseball players.

Uncle Jim explained how minor league baseball worked. "You've got your three levels: triple-A, double-A, and single-A. Triple-A is the highest level and is full of guys hoping to make it to the majors, or 'the show,' as they call it. Single-A is the lowest rung of the ladder, filled mostly with young players who were signed right out of high school or college. This is the first step of their baseball career, and for many, it's also their last. Only two out of ten of those guys will ever get to the show."

We walked into the stadium, and I was struck by how small it was. There were only 3,000 seats, and they were all very close to the field. The entire outfield wall was one big billboard. It was covered with ads from Gino's Pizza Palace, Earl's Auto Body, and Mrs. Butterworth's baby-sitting service. It was a far cry from the major league stadiums with their 50,000 seats, luxury boxes, and giant video screens. Yet there was something very cool about this ballpark, where you could sit close enough to actually see the players' faces.

Uncle Jim led us down the aisle to the first row behind the dugout. The Cubs were on the field, doing stretching exercises as a coach with a big beer gut yelled out instructions.

"This is a great bunch of guys," he said. "Some real characters, too. Every player on the team gets a nickname, usually the first week he gets here. And he's gonna be stuck with that nickname forever. It'll follow him the rest of his career. The name usually has to do with a personal trait of some kind, and some of them are very appropriate. Take that guy, for example."

Uncle Jim pointed to Eddie Cortez, a shortstop from Cuba, who was nicknamed Reptile. Eddie's was a great story. Like all players, he was superstitious. But even for a baseball player, Eddie was a little crazy.

In his first game, Eddie was in the on-deck circle when a lizard paid him a visit. Eddie put the lizard down his shirt and went up to bat. As the poor, confused lizard wiggled around inside his shirt, Eddie wiggled around with it, prompting laughter from both dugouts and the 212 fans watching.

Eddie hit the first pitch over the right field wall for his first professional home run, and he gave all the credit to the lizard. And from that game on, he always put the lizard down his shirt when he came up to bat. His teammates nicknamed him Reptile, and a minor league legend was born.

Then there was Darnell Hope. Darnell, a black kid drafted out of a small high school in Georgia, didn't look a day older than me. He was always smiling, a bundle of energy with a look that said he still couldn't believe he was there.

"Talented kid," Uncle Jim said. "Great speed, good glove, and if he can learn to hit the curveball, you might see him on a baseball card someday."

The guys called Darnell Hope "Hopeless," which Darnell took pretty well, laughing along with his teammates. He teased them right back, saying they'd all better take their shots now because he didn't plan on staying around too long.

Uncle Jim's favorite player was Luke Crane. At age 32, Luke was the oldest guy on the team, so his nickname was Geezer. Luke had been in the minors for 12 years and never made it past double-A, but he just couldn't stop playing. The Cubs were nice enough to keep him around, and Uncle Jim said they'll eventually make him a coach.

"Geezer's the real thing, a throwback to the days when this was still a game. He knows damn well he'll never make it beyond Oshkosh, never make any real money, but Luke's here for the pure joy of playing."

A big goofy-looking guy with red hair limped over to us. "That's Kevin Couch, our first baseman," Uncle Jim said. "That kid's the most injury-prone human I've ever seen. First day with us, he bangs his head getting on the team bus. Then he sits down on someone's open pocket knife. Needed 12 stitches in a place you never want to get them. That's how Kevin Couch got the name Kevin Ouch."

"What is it this time, Ouch?" Uncle Jim asked.

"It wasn't my fault, Jim. Cortez was chasing me with that lizard, and when I ran away, I pulled a calf muscle. Rub it out for me, will ya?"

Kevin propped his foot up on the dugout roof and moaned as Uncle Jim massaged his calf. After a minute, Uncle Jim's skillful hands had worked out the cramp, and Kevin ran back onto the field. He turned around to Uncle Jim, saying, "You're the best, man!" That's when he tripped over a batting helmet and sprained his ankle. The other players laughed and chanted, "Ouch! Ouch! Ouch!" Brad and I cracked up.

As the players started fielding practice, Uncle Jim tossed us an equipment bag. "Grab a glove, get out there, and show me what you got."

"Alright!" Brad said, with a big grin. Easy for him to smile—he could actually *play* baseball. Sure enough, Brad got out there at shortstop and cleanly fielded five ground balls.

"Not bad for a rookie," Eddie Cortez said, impressed. Then he pointed at me. "Why don't you take second base, kid?"

I went out to second base, which just happened to be my position on our softball team back home. But this place was light years from our undersized field. We were on a regulation-size field where the bases were 90 feet apart, and to me, home plate looked like it was six blocks away.

I barely had time to catch my breath before the coach hit the first ground ball my way. It was an easy roller, and I charged the ball, feeling really good about it, right until it rolled under my glove and off into right field.

That's when Eddie Cortez came over to me. "Hey, kid, didn't anybody ever show you how to vacuum?" he asked.

"How to *what*?"

"Vacuum. You know, suck up ground balls."

Since nobody had, Eddie took the next 10 minutes and showed me the proper way to field ground balls. He taught me exactly how to move my feet, depending on where the ball was hit. He showed me how to get down on the ball and get my glove in front of it. It made all the difference. I relaxed and fielded six balls in a row. The throw to first was a lot longer than I was used to, but after bouncing a few, I adjusted to the distance. With Brad at short and me at second, the coach asked us to "get two," meaning to turn the double play. It was so cool, especially being the pivot man and making the throw to first. But the real fun started when we went to the outfield.

Catching fly balls is not as easy as it looks, especially when they're hit with a fungo bat, an extra long, skinny bat designed solely to hit high fly balls.

Brad and I trotted out to left field, and one of the coaches hit us some flies. I wisely let Brad go first. The coach skillfully swung under the ball and hit the highest fly I'd ever seen. Brad looked up, stepped back, and then stepped forward. But the ball sailed five feet over his head.

"Harder than it looks, isn't it, jock boy?" I teased.

"Like you're Derek Jeter now?" Brad shot back. "You won't even get near the ball."

"Oh, yeah? Five bucks says I catch it."

"You're on!"

I have no idea why I ever got so cocky, especially since I'd never played the outfield much. Actually, they'd stuck me in right field for a couple of games, but I'd never had a fly ball hit my way. But my adrenaline was pumping, and even the slightest chance to show up my brother must have pushed some button inside that told me, "I can do this."

Before I could think about what I'd gotten myself into, I heard the crack of the fungo bat. The ball rocketed into the hazy sky like a space shuttle launch, and then it just disappeared.

This ball was hit a lot higher than Brad's, and even a few of the Cubs started to "ooh" and "ahh." "That's a rainmaker!" Kevin Couch shouted.

I had no clue where the ball was and even less where it was going to come down. But I bit my lip and did what I always do under pressure—I broke out into uncontrollable laughter.

As the ball started coming down, I tried to track it, dancing around in circles and giggling like an idiot. I was less concerned about catching the stupid ball than I was about having it crack my skull and smash my brain. I figured I'd need my brain—at least until I got through high school.

The ball was falling faster now, and I was laughing even harder. I took a few steps to my left. But then I realized it was dropping a few steps to my right. I ran there and stuck my glove on top of my head, purely in self-defense. Then I lost my balance and fell backward on my butt—and the ball miraculously landed right in my outstretched glove.

That's when the team went wild, cheering and shouting. They lifted me up like I'd just hit the winning home run in the World Series. Brad was as red as a tomato, and I fully expected steam to come out of his ears. I shrugged like it was no big deal, and he grudgingly handed me his five-dollar bill.

Darnell Hope ran up to me, shaking his head. "That's the ugliest catch I've ever seen, kid. And what the hell was so funny? You sounded like a hyena out there."

The other players instantly started chanting: "Hyena! Hyena! Hyena!" And that's how I earned my Cubs nickname. For the rest of the day, Hyena was my new name.

One of the coaches shouted toward the outfield, "All

right, ladies, batting practice!" This is always the team's favorite part of the day.

Brad and I stood behind the batting cage and watched each player each step in for 10 swings. Before they'd begun practice, each guy had put 10 bucks into a hat. The cash would be the prize in a contest. Whoever cranked the longest home run would win a hundred bucks out of the hat. But if anyone hit the Gino's pizza sign on the left field wall, he'd win *all* the money. Since no one had ever hit the Gino's sign and won all the money, there was a lot left in the old hat.

To make matters easier, one of the Cubs' starting pitchers stood on the mound and threw big, easy strikes over the plate.

But the best part of this ritual was the sideshow, most of it coming from the dugout. Whenever a batter was up, the rest of the team razzed, distracted, and taunted him like nothing I'd ever heard before.

"You suck!" "You couldn't hit your mother!" And that was just the tame stuff. Some of the guys used words I haven't heard since my Dad dropped that case of motor oil on his foot.

Kevin Couch launched a shot deep into the last row of the bleachers, and so far his was the longest home run. Darnell Hope was the last batter up. No one had come close to hitting the smiling Gino on that pizza sign.

Now the entire team started in on him, louder and meaner than ever. A couple of the guys spit sunflower seeds at Darnell just as he swung. But he didn't get rattled by it. He kept his cool, cursing them back, but never took his eyes off the ball.

Then, on the eighth pitch, Darnell hit a screaming line drive right toward the pizza sign. There was total silence as everyone watched the ball sail smack into Gino's head. Darnell went crazy then, laughing and shouting and whooping.

"I guess there's hope for Hopeless after all! Thanks for the rent money, suckers!"

Darnell grabbed the hat with the cash, put it on, and did a frenetic victory dance all around the bases. Nobody'd ever hit Gino before, making Darnell an instant Oshkosh Cubs legend.

Suddenly, we were startled by two loud claps of thunder. Everyone looked up at the sky as rain started to fall. It started as a little sprinkle, but soon it was beating down harder, like nothing I'd seen before. These drops were so heavy, they actually stung when they hit you. We get a lot of rain in San Francisco, but it's never anything like this.

"Welcome to the Midwest, boys," Uncle Jim said. "Sometimes these early summer rains can become torrential."

The players grabbed all their equipment and tossed it into the dugout, then rolled the batting cage under the grandstand.

Brad and I followed the guys into the dugout, but by then we were already soaked. The players seemed happy that practice was over, but nobody was moving to leave. Instead, they just stood there, watching the downpour.

As we stood under cover in the dugout, the infield got muddier by the minute. Some little lakes were already forming.

"Give it about 10 minutes," Eddie said, smiling. Ten minutes till what? I wondered.

When the infield was a totally muddy swamp, the players raced out to the base paths. Like little kids playing a game of slip-and-slide, they frolicked in the mud.

Most of the guys started at second base, ran full speed around third, and then belly-slid into home. They were laughing and shouting like 10-year-olds. I'd never seen adults have that much fun.

Brad and I looked at each other. Then we bolted out of the dugout to join the madness. I was up to my ankles in water the instant I hit the field. I ran past first base toward second, trying to stay upright on my slipping and sliding feet. After a normal slide into second, I skidded on my right side as water and mud sprayed me from head to toe.

Meanwhile, Brad made a spectacular belly flop across home plate, bringing cheers from the whole team. By the time he got to his feet, he looked like a six-foot, chocolate-covered candy bar. The only way you could recognize him was by his teeth when he smiled.

As for me, now that I'd gotten myself wet, I was ready for my head-first slide into home. Several players gathered around the plate and started chanting my nickname, encouraging me to slide on in. "Hyena! Hyena! Hyena!" they called, which really got me pumped.

I took off full speed from third and never slowed down. About 20 feet from the plate, I got ready, preparing for launch. Springing forward, I practically flew through the air with both hands straight out in front. Then I slid with such force that I shot 10 feet past the plate, right into a big pool of mud.

Mud flew into my mouth, and I choked a little from laughing so much. I probably had 10 pounds of mud in my underwear alone, and everything felt kind of squishy. The guys picked me up and slapped me on the back for my efforts. Then Brad came over, laughing, and gave me a big muddy hug.

Uncle Jim hosed us down before letting us back in his truck. It felt good to get the mud off, but it would take a few long showers to feel completely clean again. We rode home in our wet underwear, the truck's heater warming our shivering legs. Brad and I just sat there, grinning.

We didn't talk for a while, but then Brad summed it all up for us both: "That was one stone-cold, fun day. Thanks a lot, Uncle Jim."

"My pleasure, Brad," Uncle Jim said, smiling at Brad's choice of words.

It was a day I'll definitely never forget. I guess there actually was stuff to do in old Oshkosh after all.

8

The Girl in the Car

The next day, Uncle Jim showed us around town. The rain had stopped, and the clouds cleared as a huge rainbow glowed in the sky.

As we drove into the little town of Berlin, it felt like we'd stepped back in time. This was a real old-fashioned neighborhood. The streets were clean, the lawns were tidy, and the small houses all in a row reminded me of a Monopoly board.

Kids rode their bikes in packs, fathers and sons played catch on front lawns, and every block had some kind of yard sale. I was really struck by the quiet. There were no big city noises in Oshkosh: no sirens, no horns, and no jack-hammers. All we could hear was the sound of a solitary hedge trimmer—something you'd never even notice back home.

"Welcome to Middle America, guys," Uncle Jim said as he turned up Main Street and parked. We got out and walked around, looking in the windows of the stores and shops. Main Street was made up of funky old brick buildings, some of them built in the early 1900s, according to Uncle Jim. The fancy coffee shop was once a black-smith's shop—not something you see every day. In fact, an assortment of old horseshoes still hung on the walls.

Uncle Jim waved at neighbors, greeting them all by name, and he proudly introduced us as his nephews from California. There was definitely something different about this place. It seemed really safe and friendly.

Brad didn't say much, but his eyes lit up when we came to a park where a bunch of high school kids were playing basketball.

"Okay if I stop and play for a while?" he asked.

"Sure, Brad. Go for it. Andy and I'll meet you in an hour or so, how's that?"

"Great, Uncle Jim. Thanks." Brad sprinted across the street and watched the action, waiting to get in on the next game.

Uncle Jim and I walked around for a while and pretty much covered Main Street. When we wound up back at the truck, Uncle Jim had another good idea.

"Andy, my boy, I think it's time you tried some genuine Wisconsin custard."

"You might be able to talk me into it," I said, with a grin.

We walked down the block to this brick building where a line stretched out the door and onto the sidewalk. The place was called Custard's Last Stand, and it offered 15 flavors of Wisconsin custard, along with 30 toppings. There were a few tables inside and more on the sidewalk, but not an empty seat in either place. As we filed in at the end of the line, Uncle Jim smiled at me.

"I'm really glad you're here, Andy."

"Me, too," I said. "Seems like a very cool town."

"It is. You get a certain feeling here that's hard to explain. People care about each another. They really try to help each other out, and they don't even need to be asked. And there's a lot to be said for the slower pace here, too. Nobody's runnin' anybody over just trying to get to work, like in a big city. I've lived all over the country, but I'll tell you, I never really felt like I was home until I came here."

The line moved quickly, and I looked up at the flavors posted on the wall. I decided to go with the strawberry/banana custard, a swirl of each poured into a large sugar cone.

"Great choice, kid," Uncle Jim said. "Believe me, you've never tasted anything like this." He was right. The Wisconsin custard was rich and creamy, and fresher than anything I'd ever tried before. The cream probably came from one of the cows we'd passed on the way over there.

While Uncle Jim stopped in at the tobacco shop next door, I waited outside and worked diligently on my custard, which was piled high above the cone.

I had to squint in the bright midday sun, and as my eyes adjusted, I looked to my left and there, sitting in the passenger seat of a green SUV, was the most incredible-looking girl I'd ever seen. It wasn't just her light brown hair, which glistened in the sun. It wasn't just that she looked like Jennifer Aniston. It wasn't that tan, athletic-looking arm hanging out the open window that made her so amazing. No, it was those eyes. This girl had the most hypnotic eyes I'd ever seen. Green, warm, and friendly, those eyes were looking directly at me!

And she wasn't just looking. No, she actually was *smiling* at me. I smiled back, praying that I didn't have a gob of custard on my upper lip. Feeling a little silly just standing there and staring, I started walking as if I had somewhere to go. I walked slowly and tried very hard to be cool. I quickly glanced back, and she was still smiling at me. I smiled back and kept walking, not taking my eyes off her. A woman, her mom, I guessed, got into the car and pulled out in my direction. The girl nodded at me and gave me a little wave.

This was getting interesting. I nodded, waved back as cool as I could, and—BANG! I walked right into a lamp-post.

The custard cone flipped out of my hand, splattered all over my shirt and pants, then plopped on the ground. I immediately began looking for a giant hole I could disappear into.

The girl covered her eyes with her hands, like she'd just witnessed a bad accident. Then she started to laugh, but it wasn't a mean laugh, more like a feeling-sorry-for-you laugh. Either way, I was totally humiliated.

As the car went by, all I could manage was a weak shrug. Then, she did the most unexpected thing. She waved and smiled like nothing had happened. And then she was gone.

Uncle Jim was now standing a few feet away, chuckling.

"You saw that?"

"The whole thing."

"Could I have looked any more stupid?"

"Probably not. But hey, it's happened to every guy one time or another. That's the power women have over us. Laura's something, isn't she?"

"Wait. You know that girl?" I asked.

"Sure. Everybody knows her. She's our town celebrity."

"What do you mean?"

"That's Laura Kearns. She's kind of famous. She's a piano prodigy. Been playing in concerts around the world since she was eight years old."

"Wow."

"How'd you like to meet her?"

"Yeah, right. Like I'm ever going to be able to face her again after that. I'm not even going to be able to eat custard ever again."

"Come on, Andy. You fall off the horse, you get right back on."

"I'm from the city," I reminded him. "We fall off a horse, we take the bus."

"Okay, suit yourself. But if you change your mind, Laura's going to be a guest on my radio show tomorrow night."

Man, I wished he hadn't said that.

9
Laura

The next night, I was a wreck, full of jumbled feelings. Uncle Jim left at about 7:00 p.m. for the radio station, going off to interview the girl of my dreams. I wanted to go, but I just couldn't, still thinking about that custard nightmare and what a loser I must've looked like.

This Laura girl was a sophisticated professional musician. She'd been all over the world and hung out with famous people. My only musical talent is the ability to play "Yankee Doodle" on my armpit. There was no way she was going to think I was the least bit interesting. I just couldn't bring myself to face her.

To make matters worse, Brad had become fast friends with two guys he'd met playing basketball. He'd spent the last night hanging with them and was out with them again tonight.

So there I was, stuck in the house with Aunt Karen and that weird dog, Clyde. We were playing Scrabble, and Clyde was snuggling up against me, with one of his paws on my leg.

"He seems kind of needy tonight," I said, as Aunt Karen spelled the word *zephyr* for 42 points.

"Actually, Andy, I think Clyde senses that *you* might need some extra attention."

Just as I was thinking about how ridiculous that sounded, Clyde picked up his head, cocked it to one side and whimpered. The dog was agreeing with her. Karen definitely had this thing with animals.

"Don't worry about me, guys, I'm fine," I assured them.

"Who are you kidding, buster?" Aunt Karen asked. "You think I just fell off a turnip truck? Actually, I *did* fall off a turnip truck once, but that's another story. My point is, you and I both know that you want to see Laura again."

You just couldn't fool her.

"Okay, I do want to see her, but I can't. I just can't."

Aunt Karen sprang to her feet, startling me and the dog. "Look, you had an embarrassing moment. Custard happens! Get over it! Don't let some stupid mishap keep you from what might be your destiny. Life is all about following your heart. So get off your butt and go for it!"

If that wasn't persuasive enough, Clyde barked his agreement and took my sleeve in his mouth, yanking on it until I was on my feet. I swear that dog was more human than my brother.

"All right, all right. Can you drive me to the radio station?"

Aunt Karen smiled. "You've got four minutes to get dressed."

The radio station was 10 minutes away, hardly enough time to get a classical music education, but bless her heart, Aunt Karen tried. She drilled my head with so many names and movements that by the time I got there, I didn't know Chopin from "Chopsticks." I did learn the Italian word for real fast, *allegro*. That's exactly how my heart was beating by the time we got to the station.

Aunt Karen and I walked into the studio and found Uncle Jim and Laura in a small glass-enclosed booth. They sat in swivel chairs in front of microphones, each of them wearing headphones, while Uncle Jim monitored the sound levels on a small board in front of him.

Laura looked beautiful. Her hair was a little more done up, and she wore a sweater that really brought out the color of her green eyes. Aunt Karen and I listened as Uncle Jim played a CD Laura had recorded with some big-time orchestra. She was doing a piano solo by Brahms. Somehow, in her crash course in the car, Aunt Karen had never got around to mentioning him.

I watched Laura carefully as she listened to her music. Her head moved slightly from side to side, and she occasionally closed her eyes. It was as if she were actually playing the piece again. Even though I hated classical music and had no idea what to listen for, I must admit that her playing was so beautiful, it totally changed how I thought about the piano.

The piece was over, and Uncle Jim leaned in toward the microphone. "That was Johannes Brahms, Piano Sonata Number 3, in F Minor. The soloist is my guest, Laura Kearns. That was beautiful, Laura."

"Thank you," she replied, with a slight blush. Laura looked even hotter when she blushed. Uncle Jim asked a few more questions, mostly about her favorite composers and her busy schedule. Before I knew it, the interview was over and they were taking off their headphones.

"You're on, Romeo," Aunt Karen said as she walked me into the interview booth. Now my heart was beating *double* allegro.

Uncle Jim was surprised to see me but wasted no time in introducing me and Laura.

"We kind of already met," Laura said, smiling.

"Yeah," I added, "I'm the one who proved it's physically impossible to walk and eat custard at the same time."

Laura laughed. I took that as a good sign, and so did my knees, which finally stopped shaking. Uncle Jim and Aunt Karen excused themselves, leaving us alone. I stood there for a few awkward seconds as neither of us spoke. Then I decided to plunge in.

"I really liked your music."

"Thanks. Are you into classical?"

"'Fraid not. Unless I'm trapped in an elevator."

She laughed again. "Well, at least you're honest. What year of high school are you in?"

"Junior." So much for my honesty. Okay, I was going to be a sophomore. No big deal, I just added one measly year.

"Me, too," Laura said, which made her a year older than me and even more exciting. "So, where are you from?"

"San Francisco. It's a pretty cool city mostly, except

73

for, you know, the earthquakes, the traffic, the fog, and the homeless—not that I have anything against the homeless. I mean, it's not their fault they're homeless, it's just that . . . I'm rambling, aren't I?"

"Yes, but I'll let it slide this time. I love San Francisco. Played there twice. Went to a 'Niners game, too."

"Get out of here. You like football?"

"Oh, I see, just because a girl plays piano, she can't like football? I'm a big Green Bay Packers fan."

"Nice," I said. This girl was getting more interesting every minute. In fact, I considered coming clean, telling her I'd lied about going into my junior year and swearing I'd never lie to her again, 'til death do us part. But then again, why take a chance on blowing it? I could play the older man if I had to. I stood up straighter and tried to make my voice sound deeper.

We talked about our schools. She only went to hers for three hours a day. Then she practiced the piano for three hours. I could only wonder what such dedication was like.

"I took saxophone lessons—twice," I said. "My career was prematurely cut short by a severe canker sore on my upper lip."

Laura laughed. "Have you thought about the drums?" she said. "Most drummers don't use their lips."

"You've obviously never seen me drum," I shot back.

Talking to her was so natural—it was like talking to one of the guys. She was so different from all the girls at school. There was absolutely no phoniness, no drama, no superiority. She was so *real*.

"How long are you staying for?" she asked.

"We're here for two weeks."

"Cool! Call me, and I'll show you around town," she said, flashing that killer smile.

"I'd like that," I said.

Then, she did something I didn't expect. She took my hand. This girl works fast, I thought. Following her lead, I locked my fingers around hers and we were holding hands. Not bad for virtual strangers. Laura giggled and then pried my hand open. She then picked up a pen and wrote her phone number on my palm. I felt like an idiot, allowing myself to think that she wanted to hold hands already.

"Promise you'll call me."

"I promise. I just hope it doesn't wear off before I get home."

"Memorize it," she said, hitting me with that smile again.

"I already have: 555-643-9287," I said, without looking.

The door opened, and her mother, who I recognized from the custard incident, entered. She was pushing something in front of her, but at that exact moment, I didn't realize what it was.

"Ready, sweetheart?"

"Mom, this is Andy. Andy, this is my mother."

The next 90 seconds were a total blur. I think I said something like "Nice to meet you," but I'll never know.

All I remember is Laura's mom positioning the wheelchair next to Laura's swivel chair, then Laura lifting herself, her face contorted with exertion as she shifted herself from the swivel chair to the wheelchair.

I never saw it coming, and I was stunned. Thinking back, I hope I didn't look or act stunned, but I probably did. My stomach got that free-fall feeling you get on a roller coaster when it starts down that first big hill.

Laura had looked so perfect sitting there. Who would've ever thought she had a disability? The girl of my dreams was unexpectedly rolling out of the room in a wheelchair.

"Talk to you soon, Andy."

"You got it."

Then she was gone. I sat there, trying not to hyper-ventilate, realizing I hadn't taken a breath for a while. I was angry, but I wasn't exactly sure about what. Then I felt guilty for being angry. Could I be any more of a jerk? I mean, she was a great-looking, bright, super-talented girl. So she couldn't walk. Did that really change anything? Being totally honest, I wasn't sure. Man, was I confused.

Uncle Jim came back into the studio.

"How'd it go?" he asked.

I just looked at him for a few seconds, thinking that if this was his idea of a joke, it was a pretty sick one.

"Andy? You all right?"

"Why the hell didn't you tell me?"

"Tell you what?"

"You know. That she's . . . in a wheelchair."

"I didn't think it was important."

"Not important?" I said, as my voice got louder and higher than I wanted it to. "I had the right to know!"

"I'm sorry. You did have the right to know. I guess I was afraid if I told you, you wouldn't agree to meet her. I never should have assumed that. I prejudged you, and I apologize."

We sat there for a while in silence.

"Maybe you were right," I said. "I don't know if I would've come if you'd told me."

"Andy, Laura's a terrific girl."

"Tell me about it. It's just that one minute she's so perfect, the next . . . "

"I'm sorry. You shouldn't have had to find out like that. Look, if you don't want to call her . . . "

"Of course I'm going to call her! What kind of a dick do you think I am?" As I said this, I started to wonder myself. Then I realized there was something I had to know, and I had to know it now.

"So what happened? Was she born with some kind of birth defect or something?"

Uncle Jim took a breath, and I tensed up as he explained. "When Laura was four, she and her father were in a car accident. They were hit by a truck driver who fell asleep at the wheel. Laura's father was killed instantly. She was paralyzed from the waist down. Knowing Laura'd never walk again, her mother steered her toward the piano, never realizing that she was a prodigy who was born to play. It was the only positive thing that came out of that terrible tragedy."

As Uncle Jim shut down the studio, I sat there, alone with my thoughts. As we walked out of the building toward the car, he put his hand on my shoulder. It was just a gesture—no big deal—but at that moment in my life, I really needed that reassuring hand.

10

Mr. Smooth

The next day, Aunt Karen and Uncle Jim took Brad and me to Lake Winnebago. The largest lake in Wisconsin, Winnebago is beautiful and crystal clear.

Uncle Jim rented a sailboat and gave us a crash course in sailing. The best part of the day was diving into the lake from the boat, but the water was 58 degrees, and I thought my heart was going to jump right out of my chest.

As much as I enjoyed the day, my mind was somewhere else. I couldn't go five minutes without thinking about Laura. I replayed the last night's highlights over and over in my head: Laura's smile . . . feeling so comfortable with her . . . our first laugh together . . . how easy it was to talk to her . . . Laura writing her phone number on my hand . . . her mom coming in with . . . the *wheelchair*. Laura getting into it and the queasy feeling I'd had when I saw her being wheeled out of the studio.

When we got home that evening, I thought about calling her. I wanted to, but I was a little scared. Sure, I had talked to girls on the phone before, but mostly about homework or high school gossip. I'd never called to ask one out on a date. I also felt a little awkward, wondering about what we would do when we went out. I mean, we couldn't exactly go roller blading. The more I thought about it, the more nervous I got, wondering how to even start the conversation.

Then it hit me. I had my own personal babe coach right in front of me: my pain in the ass of a brother, Brad. He's called tons of girls, and a lot agree to go out with him for some reason, so he must be doing something right.

I got Brad alone, sat him down, and spilled my guts. "Brad, can I pick your brain for a minute?" Now *that* was something I'd never been able to say before.

"What do you need, bro?"

"How do you call a girl and ask for a date?" Brad smiled and put his arm on my shoulder, like the wise old man he wasn't.

"Actually," he said, "most of the time, girls call me."

"You're *so* not helping."

"Okay, okay. First thing is you've got to be cool. In control. Like you've done this a thousand times before."

That made sense.

"Act like you're interested, but not too interested."

That made *no* sense.

"See, if you're too interested, you give them the upper hand. Remember, *always* keep the upper hand."

I didn't have the heart to tell him that I couldn't care less about the upper hand; I just wanted a hand that wasn't shaking when I punched in her number and made the call.

"So be cool, and act interested, but not too interested. Is that it?" I asked.

"Well, it helps if you have pecs like these," he said, flexing. I started to leave in disgust, but Brad stopped me. In a lowered voice, he said, "So, bro, do you need a condom?"

"For a phone call? I don't think so, Brad." Jeez, is he a dope sometimes.

I began psyching myself up to call Laura. The one thing that Brad said that actually seemed like good advice was to sound like I'd done this before. Since that wasn't the case, I decided to make a few notes to help me keep the conversation going. I often made notes to prepare for tests, including a science test where I named all 37 body parts of a frog and aced it. Of course, the frog was dead and just lying there. Laura would be a bit more challenging.

First on my list, I printed in big capital letters FUN TALKING TO YOU, referring to our little encounter last night. Next, I wrote WHEN'S YOUR NEXT CONCERT?—making sure I sounded interested in her life. Then I figured I should have some suggestions as to what we would do on our date, which prompted another list: MOVIE, DAIRY QUEEN, and WHAT WOULD YOU LIKE TO DO?

After studying the list and renumbering the items several times in conversational order, I was ready. I snuck off to Aunt Karen's bedroom to ensure privacy. Knowing how dry my mouth gets when I'm nervous, I put a big glass of water next to the phone. I looked at the palm of my hand, where Laura had written her number. Although it had washed off from sailing, I still had it locked in my head, like I'd promised.

I took a deep breath, then a sip of water, and, finally, dialed the number. One ring. Two rings. Then, as I leaned back on the bed, the phone cord toppled the glass over, spilling the whole glass of water on my notes. The red ink looked like dripping blood that was now staining Aunt Karen's white bedspread. Even worse, not a word on my list was legible.

"You idiot!" Unfortunately, I said this just as Laura answered the phone.

"Who *is* this?" she asked, sounding somewhat surprised.

"*You're* not an idiot. *I'm* the idiot."

"Andy, is that you?"

How'd she know? "Yes, it's me, and I just had a little accident." Very cool. Now I sounded like I'd peed in my pants. "How ya doin'?" I asked, way too cheerfully, as I tried to wipe up the ink from the bedspread.

"Are you okay? You sound strange."

"It's nothing, a long story, forget it. So . . ."

Well, I sure couldn't go to my notes. So, smooth as ever, I said, "How ya doin'?" one more time.

"I'm good. I'm really glad you called."

"Me, too. So, what's new?"

She laughed. "Since last night? Not a whole lot. What did you do today?"

I filled her in about going sailing, and she seemed pretty interested. But that only took up, like, 40 seconds. Then there was silence. It wasn't a big pause, but nobody was saying anything, so I quickly jumped in to plug the hole.

"So, when do you perform again?" I asked, not wanting my notes to be a complete waste.

"On Monday. I have a one-night gig in Chicago."

She talked about traveling and how it wasn't as glamorous as it seemed. Talking to her was pretty easy, and I loosened up, feeling silly for being so worried about it. I waited for the next pause and decided to go for it.

"So, you want to maybe do something, like maybe tomorrow night?"

"That'd be great."

Boy, was I good at this or what?

"I was thinking maybe we could go to a movie or something." A safe, honorable, time-tested date.

"I've got a better idea," Laura said. "Let's go bowling."

"You can bowl?" The instant I said it, I slapped my forehead with my hand.

"Yes, I can bowl. It's not exactly mountain climbing." Her voice had a little edge to it.

"I'm sorry. I didn't mean it like that. I guess I was just surprised, that's all."

"Hey, I can do more than you think. This walking thing is way overrated."

"Then bowling it is. But I'm not going to take it easy on you."

Laura laughed. "Good. Because I want you to bring your A game when I kick your butt."

Now I was laughing. We'd hardly met, and she was trash-talking me already. You had to like this girl.

"You wouldn't want to make it interesting, would you?" I asked.

"You mean, like, a bet? Sure. How 'bout best out of three games? Loser buys the burgers."

"You're on," I said. "Wait. How're we gonna get there?"

"My Mom'll drop us off. We'll pick you up tomorrow night at seven."

"It's a date. Well, not exactly a *date*, you know . . . "

"That's cool. You can call it a date. I'm sure a guy like you has had *lots* of dates."

"Hundreds," I said, as we both laughed at the absurdity of this. Unfortunately, she was laughing a lot harder than I was.

11

It's Not Really a Date... or Is It?

Ten minutes to seven. After rummaging through my suitcase and trying on several different combinations, I decided on black jeans and my new brown T-shirt, which, according to my mom, brought out "the sparkle in my eyes."

My mom. Funny how I hadn't thought of her or Dad until now. Here I was, about to go on my first official date, and they actually were missing it. That little ripple of sadness quickly evaporated when I walked out to the living room and saw Aunt Karen, Uncle Jim, and Brad with those silly little grins on their faces. Even Clyde looked like he was smiling.

"What?" I asked.

"The kid's first actual date!" Brad announced. "I'm tearing up here." He mockingly dabbed at his eyes.

"Give me a break, will you? It's no big deal."

"It's a *very* big deal," Aunt Karen said. "It's a rite of passage. Something you'll never forget. And that's why we must capture this moment for posterity."

"Please don't make a Kodak moment out of this, I really . . ."

Too late. Aunt Karen whipped out the camera and

started snapping away, blinding me with the flashes. A blurry Uncle Jim got up from his chair and came toward me, reaching into his pocket.

"Forgive her. She once took a picture of me while I was having an appendicitis attack."

"That's only because no one would ever believe how green you were," Aunt Karen said.

"I want you to take this, Andy," Uncle Jim said, putting a twenty in my hand. "And have a great time."

"Of course he'll have a great time. Laura's a terrific girl!" Aunt Karen said.

"I still can't believe she can bowl," Brad said, shaking his head.

"Of course she can bowl. It's not exactly mountain climbing," I said, borrowing Laura's words and hearing myself sounding even more annoyed than she had.

"Hey, lighten up, bro," Brad said. "All I meant was, you know, it's nice of you to go out with a chick who's . . . you know, handicapped and stuff."

"Well, I hang out with you, and you're *stupid* and stuff."

"What did I say?" Brad protested.

A horn blew outside, and I was relieved because I couldn't take another minute of that pre-date chatter. I thanked Uncle Jim for the money, and they all wished me a good time, even Clyde, who barked his encouragement.

Laura was sitting in the passenger seat of the green SUV, just like the first time I saw her in town. In the glow of the orange setting sun, she looked more beautiful than ever.

As I walked toward the car, I felt caught between excitement and dread. What if we ran out of things to talk about after the first 10 minutes? The first *two* minutes? And to be honest, I couldn't help thinking about the wheelchair. Was I going to have to push her around everywhere? Not that I minded, but would people be staring at us?

"Hey, Andy," Laura called cheerfully out the window.

"Hi, Laura."

"Cool shirt."

"Thanks." I made a mental note to listen to my mom more often, at least in the area of fashion. Laura's mom was nice, and we all made small talk on the brief ride to the bowling alley.

We pulled into the parking lot of Oshkosh Beer and Bowl, and Mrs. Kearns parked in a handicapped space next to the door. I got out of the car and watched helplessly as she took Laura's wheelchair from the back and set it up near the passenger seat. Laura turned her back to the open door, and Mrs. Kearns lifted her and then sat her in the wheelchair.

"Okay, honey, just give me a call when you're ready to be picked up. Have fun, you two."

"Thanks, Mrs. Kearns," I said as she disappeared into the driver's seat. I walked behind Laura so I could help push her chair. But before I had a chance, she'd propelled herself 20 feet ahead of me. I had to speed walk just to catch up. As I would quickly come to realize, this girl didn't need much help.

The bowling alley was old, built sometime in the 1950s, according to Laura. There were neon signs everywhere, each one flashing the name of a different brand of beer. There were only 16 lanes, and half of them were being used by a women's league.

The pulse of the action was at the bar, which was packed with loud people laughing and talking. Next to the bar was a small smoky room with some pool tables and a separate area with old video games.

"Is this place retro or what?" I said, taking it all in.

"Yeah, it's got a cool, Art Deco feel to it," Laura said. "On Friday and Saturday nights, it really rocks. They have laser lights, and the pins glow in the dark."

I went up to the counter, where a dopey-looking boy with a face full of zits stood. I guessed he was 17, but he acted like he owned the place.

"Can we get a lane, please?" I asked.

"You got it, ace."

Ace. And he said it so sarcastically.

"Shoe size?" he asked.

"Nine." I then instinctively turned to Laura. "Laura, what size shoe . . . " The look on her face stopped me cold. Did I just ask a paralyzed girl what size bowling shoe she wore? Could I be a bigger idiot?

"Laura, I'm sorry. It just kind of slipped out."

"It's okay, Andy. Don't worry about it."

But it wasn't okay. I felt awful, even if Laura was cool about it. I turned back to zit boy, who was now smiling at me.

"Smooth," he said.

"No one asked you. Just give me my shoes."

He took a pair of size nines and slammed them down on the counter, barely missing my thumb. I gave him my meanest scowl, more for Laura's benefit than his.

"I'm going to get my ball," Laura said. I figured she was going to go over to the rack of balls and pick one. Instead, she rolled over to a wall of lockers. After turning a combination lock, she took out a black leather bag with a handle.

"Whoa. You have your own bowling ball?"

"Yeah, is that like, illegal, or something?"

"No, no, you just never mentioned you're a hustler."

Laura laughed. "Oh yeah, that's me. Concert pianist by day, bowling hustler by night. You're not wimping out on our bet, are you?"

"'Course not. It'll just make it that much sweeter when I beat you."

"See you on Lane 16, sucker."

Laura smiled playfully and rolled away, using the ramp to get down to the alley level. I went over to the rack to pick out a ball. Most were black and weighed 16 pounds— much too heavy for me. There were some lighter orange and purple balls, but they all seemed to scream "wuss." Now I was faced with a dilemma: go with the heavy black ball I couldn't throw without giving myself a hernia or take a lighter ball—the same as the six-year-olds were using on Alley 2. I gritted my teeth and picked up a black one—this was a man's ball.

As I carried the "man's ball" toward Lane 16, I could almost hear my right arm screaming out: "Put that thing down! You're no man!" It felt like I was carrying a refrigerator with one hand. As I approached Laura, I sucked it up and smiled through the pain.

"I see you went for the heavy one," she said.

"What else?" I swung the ball a couple of times for emphasis, and almost fell over from the weight. Laura laughed as I dropped it onto the return rack with a thud.

"Go ahead." Laura motioned. "Take a practice frame."

I picked up the big black ball and carefully stepped up to the lane. It was actually getting heavier, somehow. Then I tried to remember my old form, not having bowled since my seventh birthday. Was it four steps and throw off my right foot, or five steps and throw off my left foot?

I took a few steps toward the pins and then swung my arm back far enough to make sure I got something on the ball. Well, I got something on it, all right. The ball flew out of my hand on the back swing, bounced a couple of times, and rolled toward Laura, who was sitting at the scorer's table. She had this deer-in-the-headlights look, not knowing whether to laugh or scream.

"Oops." It was the only thing I could offer.

"I'm not going to have to wear a helmet, am I?" Laura teased. Then, "Why don't you try my ball? It's only 12 pounds," she offered.

I picked up Laura's ball, which was a beautiful shade of aqua blue. The finger holes were a little small, but it felt a lot better than that cannonball I'd started with.

"Thanks," I said.

"Hey, I want you to be comfortable . . . and I want to survive this date."

"Very funny. You ready? Let the games begin," I said. "Would you like to go first?"

"No, you're the guest. Show me what I'm up against."

Not too much pressure there. I stepped up to the lane with Laura's ball, took a deep breath, and started to focus. I could see that this girl was pretty competitive, and I was determined to beat her. I rolled, and the ball went right down the middle, hitting the pocket and knocking down nine pins.

I walked back to the ball rack and met Laura's eyes, which seemed to say "Not bad." I stepped back up to the lane and took dead aim at the seven-pin in the corner. I released the ball a bit too hard, and it curved past the pin—right into the gutter.

"Good try," Laura said, as she rolled past me to Lane 16. Just how was this girl going to bowl? I wondered. I watched anxiously as Laura went to the ball rack. She picked up her ball and cradled it in her lap, then rolled to the far left side of the lane. Next, she took the ball with her right hand and hung her arm over the side of the chair.

Using her left arm to propel the chair, Laura then started rolling toward the foul line, picking up speed as she went. Just before she got there, she pulled her right arm back and released the ball. It started out on the right side of the lane, but then it began to curve toward the pocket like a spinning aqua blue top.

I was blown away by her power as the ball crashed into the right pocket, sending the pins flying. It was a perfect, clean strike. I sat there in awe, and at least had the presence of mind to close my gaping mouth before Laura turned around and saw it.

"Great shot."

"Thanks. It felt good leaving my hand."

As I stepped up for my second frame, I was still amazed by how good Laura was at this game, and I realized how hard she must have worked to get there.

Then I promptly threw my next ball way to the left, knocking down only one pin. Enough amazement. I had to focus here.

It took me five frames to get my rhythm, but then I got into a groove. Laura rolled only one more strike, but she picked up a few spares and scored a 132, beating me by 12 pins.

"That's one," she said, a little smugly.

"I'm a little rusty. It's been a while since I bowled." Then, with my best game face, I said, "But this time I'm going to beat you."

Laura started to laugh.

"What?"

"Nothing. You're cute when you're determined."

"I am *not* cute," I said, which made her laugh even harder.

Then it hit me as I stepped up to the lane for the next game: Laura was flirting with me. She was pretty good at it, too. I wondered if I should flirt back, but I didn't have a clue how. And what if she *wasn't* flirting, but only trying to psych me out? Well, whatever it was she was doing, she was doing a pretty good job of it.

I took a deep breath, determined not to let Laura mess with my head.

The second game was mine from the start. With laser-like concentration, I hit three strikes and three spares for a very solid 152. It was good enough to beat Laura by 25 pins, but more important, it gained me some respect. Now Laura seemed to look at me with a different attitude; that little flirting thing stopped as she put on her game face. You could tell that this girl didn't like to lose.

"Chalk up one for me," I said, in the same tone of voice she had used after winning her game.

"Great game, Andy. You really cleaned my clock. Guess we have to play one more for the tiebreaker."

"Oh, yeah. But let's get something to drink first."

We went over to the vending machines, where I bought us a couple of sodas. Laura rolled over to the viewing area, and I sat down next to her.

"So where'd you learn to bowl like that?" I asked.

"When I was eight, a friend of mine had her birthday party here. I sat there, watching all the kids get up and bowl, and even though they were all pretty nice to me, I felt stupid just sitting there keeping score. You know, who wants to be the geek in the chair? I promised myself I would never go to another bowling party unless I could bowl, too.

"So my mom did some research—she's good at that— and found a wheelchair bowling league in Madison. We went to watch one night, and I met this amazing woman named Marcie, who had lost both legs to diabetes. She'd taught herself how to bowl in her chair. And she didn't just bowl. She averaged 165."

"Wow."

"Marcie agreed to teach me to bowl, but first I had to

build up my arms. That took months of working with weights and a personal trainer. My mom kind of freaked, thinking I was going to hurt my fingers and not be able to play the piano. But it actually strengthened my hands, and I ended up with more stamina at the keyboard. Anyway, I owe it all to Marcie."

I just sat there, speechless, thinking about how incredible she was.

"What?" she said.

"Nothing," I lied. "Ready for that third game?"

"Let's do it," she smiled.

"It doesn't get any better than this, folks," I announced in my best sportscaster voice. "This is for all the marbles, winner take all. It's gut-check time."

"Can we 86 the announcing, please?"

"Oooh," I said. "Do I detect a touch of nerves?"

"Not a chance," Laura said, cool as a contract killer.

She positioned her wheelchair and threw a pretty good ball, but it hit the head pin directly, giving her the dreaded 7-10 split.

"Damn it!" Laura gritted her teeth.

Whoa. She was even more competitive than I thought. And somehow it made her even more attractive. It also made me want to beat her even more.

"Tough break," I said, insincerely.

The game was close from the start. I scored two spares and a strike, and Laura rolled two strikes in a row. At the end of six frames, she was ahead by four pins. She kept the pressure on in the seventh frame, picking up a difficult spare.

"This is getting interesting," she said, as she rolled past me.

I stepped up to the lane and rolled a perfect strike.

"*Very* interesting," I said, smiling back at her. Then the fun really began.

"Who's gonna crack first?" Laura said, in full psych-out mode.

"Not me," I shot back.

"We'll see."

Laura got another spare in the eighth frame, leaving her with 110. I matched her spare and had 109. Then, in the ninth frame, Laura missed an easy spare. She scrunched her face up into a ball of frustration and hit the arm of her wheelchair. A strike or a spare for me in the ninth would pretty much clinch it for me.

I picked up my ball and looked at Laura, who by now was all smiles.

"What?"

"It's all yours, Andy. One measly little spare and you win. Take your time now. Blow this, and you'll never live it down."

"Are you finished?"

"For now," she laughed.

But she wasn't going to psych me out. No way. I made my approach, rolled and hit the pocket, leaving only three pins. I dried my fingers on the air blower as I waited for the ball, making sure I didn't even look at her. For some reason, that ball seemed to take forever. Meanwhile, I told myself it was just an easy spare, that I only had to hit the pin in the middle.

But the second I let it go, I knew I'd missed it. The ball curved too far to the right, nicking just one pin.

"Darn," Laura said, as sincerely as she could. It was all she could do to keep from breaking into song.

"I'm just trying to keep it interesting," I said.

"I appreciate that—I was getting so bored."

So there we were: we'd been bowling for an hour and a half, and going into the tenth frame of the last game, Laura led me by two pins, 135 to 133.

"Tenth frame. This is it. It's yours to lose, Laura. Whatever you do, don't choke."

Laura chuckled and wiped her hands on her towel. Then she rolled up to the lane. She gave herself a mighty push and rolled even faster than before. Then, releasing the ball with great power, she sent it right for the pocket.

I was sure it would be a strike, but to my delight, when the pins crashed and were swept away, two were still standing. They were the six- and the ten-pin, the baby split. Even though this was the easiest split to make, it wasn't a sure thing.

As Laura rolled back, I could see the sweat beads on her forehead and upper lip. She wiped her face with her towel, dried her fingers on the blower, and picked up her ball from the return rack.

Laura slowed down this time, needing less power and more accuracy. The ball rolled right on target, but at the last second it veered, hitting only the six-pin and leaving the ten-pin still standing. Now she had nine pins, for a final score of 144, very respectable—and very *beatable*.

With my 133, all I needed was a spare. That would

give me 143, plus any pins I got on my last ball. I was in the driver's seat, and despite the temptation, I decided not to rub it in.

"That was a great try," I said.

Laura shook her head, not exactly sharing my assessment.

I stepped up to the lane and rolled a very solid ball, leaving only the five-pin, the one right in the middle. It's the easiest spare to make, and I wasn't about to miss it. Taking a deep breath, I calmly rolled the ball as straight as I could, and I had it all the way.

"Nice shot," Laura said.

Now I had one more ball and had to knock down just two pins to beat Laura. I could do this with my eyes closed.

"Two pins, Andy, that's all you need."

"I know."

I stepped up to the lane.

"Are your hands shaking?"

"You wish," I said.

"Just two little pins," Laura reminded me again.

"Do you mind?"

She backed off.

I told myself that I just had to throw it down the middle, anywhere but in the gutter, and I'd win.

I picked up the ball and started my approach. Three steps in, I heard this voice from my left.

"Don't choke, Andy."

I glanced over, and there was Laura rolling full speed down the lane next to me. It was one of the strangest and funniest sights I've ever seen. She was making this ridiculously silly face and looked like a complete idiot. And then

I just lost it. I burst out laughing and dropped the ball, bouncing it into the gutter. Laura looked back to see it and screamed in delight. Then she shrieked, "I won! I won!"

But her celebration was cut short. She was rolling too fast to stop, and her momentum propelled her chair smack into the pins in the next lane.

She screamed in amusement and somehow managed to stay in the chair. I ran down the lane after her without even thinking, sliding all the way down on the well-oiled wood.

"I had the game locked," I said. "That was *so* not cool."

"Hey, it's just a game."

"Look who's talking. Tell that to your ego."

"Okay, okay, you won. Now can you help me get out of here?"

The automatic pin-setting machine had caught the wheel of her chair. And if this wasn't embarrassing enough, a frantic voice announced over the P.A., "Maintenance to Lane 15! We have two idiots on Lane 15!"

All of a sudden, it got very quiet in the bowling alley. I turned around to see the entire place staring at us and pointing. A burly maintenance guy ran toward us, his tool belt jingling against his big stomach.

"Laura, what the heck are you doing?" he exclaimed.

"Sorry, Matt, I guess I got a little carried away."

The guy freed Laura's chair from the automatic pin setter, then she turned around calmly and started rolling off the lane. I walked alongside her, certainly the more embarrassed of the two idiots.

97

"You're nuts, you know that?" I grinned.

"Oh, yeah." She smiled.

And she *was* a little nuts. And at that moment, I wished that I could only be that nuts—so spontaneous, so free. Laura was way different from any other girl I'd ever met. She was a true original.

12

If You Havn't Ridden in
a Hearse, Don't Knock It

"Where are we going?" I asked, as I tried to keep up with Laura, who was cruising down the street at warp speed.

"You won, and I'm buying the burgers. Now, we can't eat in the bowling alley . . . unless you want to be poisoned. There's this great place up the street."

The evening air was starting to cool, and even though it was almost 9 p.m., the sky still had streaks of light. It was the best time of summer—the beginning—when the days are long and the possibilities endless.

Buddy's Burger Barn was just that, an old barn converted into a burger shop. A giant plastic cow stood by the door, with the restaurant menu brightly painted on its side. There were tables inside and out, but almost everyone was eating outside.

Lots of kids were there, and Laura seemed to know them all. She introduced me as "My friend Andy," which sounded kind of cool. We ordered two burgers, along with fries and shakes, then found our own little spot away from the crowd.

Laura raised her cup for a toast.

"To the bowling champion. Congratulations!"

"Thanks," I said, clicking her strawberry shake with my chocolate one. "That was a great match. And a lot of fun."

"Yeah, it was a kick."

"So, have you always been so competitive?"

"Am I competitive?" Laura asked.

"No, you're possessed."

Laura laughed. "I guess you can say I'm competitive. I think it comes from piano. You know, all those years of lessons, practice, and recitals. I won my first competition when I was nine, then I kept winning and winning. I never realized how much I liked winning until the first time I lost.

"It took me a while to see that it was okay to lose, to come in second. Since then, I've tried to lighten up about it. I used to practice five hours a day, but now it's down to only three."

"I can't even imagine that kind of dedication."

"It's not that big of a deal. You get so into it, you don't even notice the time." She took another sip of her drink. "So, Andy, what's your thing? What are you good at?"

"Me? Nothing. Nothing really stands out. I'm pretty ordinary in everything."

"Get out."

"No, really. I'm a boring 'B' student, a decent athlete, no special talents. I can't say I'm really great at anything."

"You're being way too modest. You have a gift."

"I do?"

"Yes. You're really funny."

100

"No, Chris Rock is really funny. I'm just ordinary funny."

I blew the wrapper off my straw, and it arched through the air, landing in a woman's hair at the next table. Laura cracked up.

"See what I mean? You're really funny."

"Yeah, I'm a real genius with a straw wrapper."

"So, genius, tell me about your brother."

"Boy, you really must be bored," I said.

She laughed. "No. I'm curious. I'm an only child, so I'm interested in that kind of stuff. Do you guys get along very well?"

"Actually, less and less. He's got major attitude. You know, like he knows everything? And the thing is, he doesn't know anything. Sometimes he can be a real tool."

"Sorry. So . . . why'd he run away?"

"You heard about that?"

"In a small town like this one, we hear about everything."

"Yeah, I guess you do. Wow. How do I explain Brad? He's done some really stupid things, but he really outdid himself this time. My Uncle Jim got him good, though. He borrowed some guy's chicken truck and . . . wait, you've heard about this part, too, haven't you?"

"Well, no, not really," she said. "At least not from anybody who was there."

I gave Laura the blow-by-blow account, which she loved.

"You're right, your brother's weird," Laura said. "But I wish I had a brother or sister—even a weird one. I mean, my mom and I are close and all, but sometimes it'd be fun to have someone else to share stuff with."

Laura looked out somewhere in the distance, and for the first time, I saw a hint of sadness in her face. Something told me I didn't know the half of it. This girl had probably been through a lot.

"Hey," she said, looking at her watch. "It's only 10:15. How would you like to go hear some awesome music?"

"Hey, I'm down with that."

Laura pulled out her cell and hit a number on speed dial.

"Bones? It's me, Laura. I'm here with a friend, and we'd really like to try to make the next set. Can you pick us up at Buddy's? Thanks! You're the best!"

"You know a guy named Bones?" I asked.

"Yeah. Doesn't everyone?" She laughed.

❖

Ten minutes later, a black hearse pulled up right next to our table and out stepped Ray "Bones" Jones. He was tall and very skinny, and he looked old with his shock of white hair.

Bones owned the town funeral home, which I guess explained the hearse. Laura said he was also a jazz musician and he owned a little club called The Attic.

"Bones, I'd like you to meet my friend Andy," Laura said, introducing us.

"How you doin', kid?" Bones asked, extending his big bony hand. "Get in the car. I got music to make."

As we headed toward The Attic, I looked around the hearse and couldn't help feeling a little freaked out. There was a black curtain behind me, and who knew what or who was behind it? The only people who rode in these things were either dead or members of the Addams Family.

"First time in a hearse, kid?" Bones asked.

"Yeah, and it's kinda creepy," I said.

"Could be worse. You could be the one back there in the box!" Bones cracked up, and Laura turned to reassure me.

"He's kidding—I think," she said.

The hearse rolled into the parking lot, and I saw that The Attic's name really fit, because that's exactly what it was—a small room over the first floor of the funeral home.

Bones helped Laura out of the hearse and into her chair, and the three of us went inside to take the elevator up to the second floor.

You could hear the music as soon as the elevator doors opened. The room was dark and smoky, with five or six tables in front of a small stage. Two guys were playing, and Bones, after setting us up at a table, walked onstage, picked up his bass, and joined in—all without missing a beat.

"Bones is amazing," Laura said. "He used to play with Miles Davis."

"How did you ever meet him?" I raised my voice so she could hear me over the music.

"When my father died in the accident, Bones took care of the funeral stuff. Then, when I started getting into the piano, he always encouraged me. You know, he even helped me find teachers and drove me to competitions—

things like that. He kind of became a friend of the family. My mom used to take me to hear him play. And then, when I started doing concerts, he became my biggest fan."

I'd never heard much jazz before this, but I was quickly getting into it. Bones was joined by a guy on saxophone and a drummer. They all sounded great together.

"Right now, they're just riffing—you know, improvising," Laura said. "Watch Al, the sax player. Every now and then, he'll nod his head to the other two. That's when they go off in another direction, like changing the tempo or the mood."

Sure enough, a few seconds later, Al nodded and the other guys went with him into a completely different pace. It was awesome, watching them play off each other. They were like a great basketball team, passing the ball around. Everyone seemed to know where everybody else was going to be.

The song ended to the enthusiastic applause of the 12 or so people in the place. Then Bones stepped to the front of the stage.

"Thank you. Now we'd like to do something a little more funky, and we could really use some help. What do you say, Laura?"

Everyone turned to Laura and started to applaud. I joined in, clapping the loudest. Laura looked at me, shrugged modestly, and rolled toward the stage. Laura rolled up a ramp—especially built for her—and positioned her chair in front of the baby grand piano.

Bones counted down the beat, and they broke into a fast-paced number. Laura took the lead, and was she ever amazing. Her fingers flew over the keyboard, getting more sound out of a piano than I'd ever heard before.

But the thing I'll never forget was the look on Laura's face. It was one of absolute concentration, as if she were shutting out the whole world. She may as well have been on her own planet, but whatever she was feeling, it lit up everyone in the room.

I sat there, tapping my foot, unable to take my eyes off her. This was pretty cool—a girl *I* was with actually knew an old jazz musician. And here I was, sitting in this place above a funeral home, listening to her and these guys making such amazing music.

Wisconsin was turning out way better than I'd ever expected. If I were home, I'd probably be spending the night with a couple of my geeky friends, playing Guitar Hero and stuffing my face with Cheese Puffs.

Every once in a while, there are times in your life when you can almost feel yourself growing up. This was definitely one of those moments.

❖

It was almost 2 a.m. when I got back to the house. It was the latest I'd ever stayed out alone, and it really felt good.

Using the key Aunt Karen had given me, I opened the door and walked into the dark living room, stumbling around for a while until my eyes adjusted. I felt something brush against my leg, followed by Clyde's hot breath as he came over to greet me.

"How you doin', Clyde?" I scratched him under his chin, then made my way into the kitchen, with Clyde tagging along. I poured myself a glass of milk and found the Oreos in the cupboard—the perfect end to a perfect evening.

As I crunched the cookies, Clyde looked longingly at me as he sat by my side. It was a look all dogs share when they watch humans eat—almost begging with their eyes for some of whatever you have.

"You want one, buddy?" I asked. I slipped a cookie in front of Clyde's nose. He sniffed, but didn't take it. But he still had that longing look. If he wasn't saying "Feed me," then what did he really want? But then he tilted his head to the side, as if asking me a question. It was like he wanted to know "So, how did it go tonight?"

Since I was still buzzing from the evening and needed someone to talk to, I decided to go for it.

"It was the best. The most fun I've ever had. Laura is totally amazing. Why didn't you tell me she was so cool? Wait—that's right. I think you actually tried."

Clyde made a sympathetic sound, as if he understood every word. I swear, he looked like he was smiling.

"Who the hell are you talking to?" It was Brad, who'd come in from our room.

"I'm talking to Clyde," I said, "and you're interrupting us."

"Sounds like you really hit it off with this girl."

Brad plopped himself down on the chair next to me and took a handful of cookies. It was one thing talking to the dog. At least he was sensitive and a good listener. I wasn't quite sure how much of this I wanted to share with my bone-headed brother.

"So, tell me, kid, how was it?"

"It was nice, really nice."

"It's late. What have you guys been doing all night?"

"It's a long story. We bowled. Then Laura introduced me to a guy named Bones. We rode in a hearse and then listened to some really good jazz above a funeral home."

"Yeah, right. Dude, if you don't want to tell me, fine. Just say so." He was actually indignant.

"That's what we *did*, Brad, I swear. It was an incredible night."

"You really rode in a hearse?" Brad asked, completely baffled.

"Yeah, and it was eerie, too."

"This sounds like quite a date."

Brad sat in full attention for the next 15 minutes as I described my evening. It wasn't like him to be so interested in my life. But up until now, my life had never been very interesting. Brad asked questions and actually wanted details. It was a first for him, and I enjoyed the attention.

"Wow," Brad said. "This Laura chick, she's really . . . different."

"Oh, yeah. She's funny, she's smart, and she's really easy to talk to."

"You like her, don't you?"

"Yeah."

"No, I mean you *like* her," Brad said, emphasizing the word *like* and making it sound illegal.

"I don't know. What do you mean by *like*?" I asked, putting the same emphasis on the word.

"It means you want to be with her—like, all the time."

"Well, I barely know her, but she's *so* not like the girls at school. Yeah, I definitely want to see her a lot more, but don't go printing up wedding invitations on me yet."

Brad laughed. "Good for you, buddy. I'm happy for you. I really am."

And he was. And it felt really good. As he sat there, crunching away on the cookies, I thought back to what Laura had said a couple of hours earlier—wishing for a brother or sister, no matter how weird. I guess I could understand it now.

"So, Brad, what about you? Was there ever a girl you really *liked*?"

Brad stopped crunching momentarily, and I realized I'd struck a nerve. He took a swig of my milk.

"Yeah, once. Linda Sandusky. She dumped me for some geek in her drama class. But you move on. It's no big deal."

I remembered this girl. About a year before, when she'd dumped him, Brad had gone into total freak mode, yelling at everybody and holing up in his room for a couple of weeks. I'd never realized that it really *had* been a big deal and that he'd actually gotten hurt.

"Sorry" was all I could manage. Brad cuffed me on the shoulder affectionately and got up. He was headed for bed. It was actually nice talking to him, and I didn't want it to end yet.

"You okay, Brad?"

"You mean about the Linda Sandusky thing?"

"No, about everything. We never really talked since . . . "

Brad turned a little red. "Since I took off? Yeah. I don't know, I guess I just weirded out a little. It was stupid, but I'm okay now. I met a couple of guys at the park. We've been hanging out, so . . . it's going to be okay here."

"Yeah, I'm getting that feeling, too."

"I'll bet you are, lover boy," Brad snickered as he stuck out his hand to give me five. I slapped it and watched him disappear into the hallway.

My brother and I were talking about girls. The last time we did that, we were plotting to put frogs down their shirts at camp.

13

How I Learned to Drive, or, More Accurately, Crash

I was up early the next morning, still thinking about Laura. I replayed the whole date in my head, minute by minute, like on my own personal DVD. I kept cueing up the best parts, and there were a lot of those.

I was walking into the kitchen to get some juice when I heard this strange, mystical-sounding music coming from the living room.

I poked my head in and saw Aunt Karen—all 200 pounds of her—stuffed into a bright purple leotard. She was doing yoga. At least, I think it was yoga. She was lying on her back with her legs bent, blowing these quick bursts of air from her mouth. She looked like Barney the dinosaur giving birth. It was such a comical sight that I laughed a little louder than I'd planned.

"Laugh again, and you're not gettin' breakfast."

"Sorry," I said.

"You've never seen anyone do yoga before?"

"Uh, yeah, but not like that."

Aunt Karen put her legs down and exhaled one more long breath.

"You should try this some time, Andy."

"Me?"

"Yes, you. It really centers you."

"I didn't realize I was off center," I said.

"Everybody's off center, smart ass." She sprang to her feet with amazing agility. "Touch your toes, kid."

"Excuse me?"

"You heard me. Reach down and touch your toes. And don't bend your knees."

I didn't want to do it, but the look on her face was frightening. I took a deep breath, dropped my arms, and started to reach down. Just as I was wondering what the big deal was, my back tightened up and my hamstrings started to scream. I smiled through the pain, determined to get my fingertips to my toes. I stretched as much as I could, but still came up two inches short.

"Ha! And you're a kid! You're supposed to be limber."

I grunted, lost my balance, and stumbled.

"That's pathetic," Aunt Karen added. Well, I couldn't argue with that.

"Watch this," she said. Then, standing straight as a board, she bent at the waist and reached down. Her fingers touched her toes, and then she continued until both palms were flat on the floor. I couldn't believe my eyes.

"Very impressive," I said.

"I know what you're thinking. How can a fat-ass like me do something like that?"

"It did cross my mind, but I wouldn't exactly use those words," I said.

"Let me clue you in on a little secret, Andy," Aunt

Karen said as she put an arm on my shoulder. "Just 'cause a cow has four legs, doesn't mean she can't ice skate."

I had no idea what that meant, but I was pretty sure I had never seen a cow ice skate.

"Ooo-kay," I said.

"It's an expression we use around here sometimes. It means you can't judge anybody by their appearance—cows or people."

"I hear you."

"Good," Aunt Karen said. "So, how'd it go last night?"

"How'd what go?"

"Don't be holding out on me. Your date. With Laura."

"It was . . . awesome. She's smart, funny, and a little bit nuts."

"Nuts is good! Yeah, Laura's the real deal. Are you two going to hook up again?"

I laughed. "Hook up?"

"Hey, I'm old, but I'm not an antique."

"Maybe not, but 'hook up' means to have sex."

"What? I *am* an antique. Question withdrawn."

"Yeah, I guess we'll go out again. She's totally fun to be with, you know?"

"Totally. Look, I've gotta go to the feed store. How'd you like to drive?"

"Me? But I don't know how to drive."

"Yeah, and there was a time when you didn't know how to walk, either."

"You're *really* going to let me drive?"

"Yes. Now, come on before I change my mind. Just don't ever tell your mother. She'd probably sue me."

So there I was, 10 minutes later, sitting in the driver's seat of Aunt Karen's pickup. I was going to drive. How cool was that? My friends back home would be dying of jealousy.

Aunt Karen held the keys out in front of me. I reached for them, but she pulled them back.

"Not so fast, kiddo. What's the first thing you do when you get into a car?"

"Buckle up," I said, reaching for my seat belt.

"Very good. Now do me a favor. Pay attention, keep alert, and, whatever you do, try not to kill me."

"Thanks for the vote of confidence," I said.

"Now, put your right foot on the gas pedal, then on the brake. Gas pedal, brake, gas pedal, brake. Just get the feel of those things."

I did as I was told, alternating my right foot between the two. Then she gave me the keys.

"Okay," Aunt Karen went on. "Now, put your hands on the wheel at the ten o'clock and two o'clock positions." This time she actually placed my hands in the proper positions on the wheel.

"Now, put your right foot firmly on the brake, turn the key, and start her up."

I turned the key in the ignition, the engine started, and I instantly felt the power of the truck.

"Now put it in drive, take your foot off the brake, and press down on the gas pedal—*gently*." I stepped on the gas a bit, and we started to move down the driveway.

"So far, so good," Aunt Karen said. "Now, lightly tap the brake and get the feel of stopping."

I tried this a few times as the truck rolled down the driveway toward the main road.

"All right. Time for your first turn. Look both ways, make sure no cars are coming, and turn right onto the highway."

I took a deep breath, checked for traffic, checked again, and then I made the turn. But the steering felt awkward, and I turned the wheel too far. I was heading for the ditch on the side of the road when Aunt Karen grabbed the wheel and straightened us out. She was very calm about it.

"You don't have to oversteer, Andy—the truck has power steering. Now, keep it steady, and try to stay at about 40 miles an hour."

So there I was: driving down the highway, my sweaty hands tightly clenched around the steering wheel while my right foot gently pressed on the gas, already tensing up in case I had to stop. But I was *driving*, and it felt great. I looked over to Aunt Karen and smiled.

"Well, aren't you the cat who ate the canary," she said. "Okay, I get it, you're stoked. Eyes back on the road, buster."

"This is so cool . . . and easy," I said. "Thanks a lot, Aunt Karen."

The road was deserted, but finally a car came toward us from the other direction. The guy slowed down and looked at me funny, but Aunt Karen gave him a wave and he went on. Then we came to an intersection, but it had no traffic lights or stop signs.

"Okay, slow down and hang a right here."

This time, I did a better job of turning and hardly went

out of the lane at all. Now I was on a narrow two-lane road, flanked on both sides by grazing cows. There wasn't a car in sight, and I started to relax a little.

"How does it feel?"

"Great," I said. "They should let kids drive earlier than 16."

"Oh, yeah," Aunt Karen laughed. "Maybe we should just let everyone drive when they're 11. I don't think so."

All of a sudden, from out of nowhere, a large spotted cow darted into the road about 50 feet in front of me.

"Hit the brake!" Aunt Karen yelled, scaring me more than the cow had. In fact, she'd startled me so much that I immediately slammed my foot down—but on the *gas* instead of the brake. We were now heading full speed toward that poor cow.

"Hit the brake! The brake!" Aunt Karen yelled.

I was now inches away from the cow. And I'll never forget the panicked look on its face, which seemed to say, "I can't believe I'm going to end up a Big Mac because of some 15-year-old punk who never should have been driving."

I finally found the brake, but there was no way I was going to stop in time. Luckily, my 15-year-old punk reflexes kicked in and, at the last possible second, I jerked the steering wheel hard to the left.

The truck skidded on two wheels across the road. Aunt Karen crashed against me and started screaming, which certainly didn't help. Then the truck crashed through a wooden fence into the pasture, where other innocent cows were grazing. You'd be surprised how fast cows can move when they want to. I was able to steer around them, and we finally stopped when the truck hit a huge haystack.

We were fine, but for some reason, Aunt Karen's air bag opened and pinned her back in her seat. It distorted her face like a cartoon character's, but as ridiculous as she looked, I was too scared to laugh.

"Are you okay?" I asked. She nodded under the air bag. "God, this is so embarrassing," I said.

"Tell me about it—I wet my pants."

This was more information than I needed to know. After I caught my breath, I started trying to free her from the air bag. "I am sooo sorry," I said, my hands still shaking. "That cow came from out of nowhere."

"It's okay, Andy, these things happen. You did a good job, swerving like that. We would've been really hurt or worse. And I know that cow's breathing easier, too."

"Yeah, but your truck, it's all smashed. I'll pay for it, I promise."

"Hey, it's just a truck, and we have insurance. We're both okay. And that's all that matters."

"Thanks," I said. "I can't believe you're this cool."

"Yeah, that's me, I'm *too* damn cool. Well, this is the last time I take a teenager on a joy ride. No offense, kid, but I'm driving home from here."

"Please do," I said, getting out of the truck.

So that was my first driving lesson. I had a feeling I'd be seeing that poor terrified cow in my dreams for many nights to come.

In about six months, I would be able to get my learner's permit. Having to drive in San Francisco, with all those crazy hills, was going to be scary enough. But at least I wouldn't have to dodge any cows.

14

And Then There Was

a Second Date

"Remember," Aunt Karen said, "*I'm* the one who wrecked the truck. You were never driving, right?"

"I don't know, Aunt Karen. You really don't have to do this for me."

"I'm doing it for me, kiddo. What Uncle Jim doesn't know won't hurt him. Now just do your part and play along."

As we walked into the house, Uncle Jim was eating at the kitchen table and I could feel my temperature beginning to rise.

"I had a little mishap with the truck. Cow crossed the road, and I had to swerve into a haystack. Front end's gonna need some work, honey."

"You guys all right?" Uncle Jim asked.

"Yeah," I said. "Thanks to Aunt Karen's quick reflexes."

Uncle Jim smiled and turned to her. "You let the kid drive, didn't you?"

"Damn it, Jim, how in the blazes did you know?"

"He's turning redder than a hothouse tomato over there."

Aunt Karen looked at me. "Thanks a lot, kid."

"Sorry," I said, "my parents told me never to lie."

"What do they know?" Aunt Karen snapped.

"Anything else you want to tell me?" Uncle Jim asked.

Before she could answer, the phone rang. Aunt Karen picked it up, and I was saved from further questioning.

"Andy, it's for you. It's *her*," she said, making a goofy face and giving me a thumbs-up.

"Hello."

"Hey you," Laura said on the other end of the phone.

"Hey, Laura."

Uncle Jim got up, but Aunt Karen stood there like she was nailed to the floor, waiting to hear every word. I went into the bathroom and closed the door.

"I had a really good time last night," Laura said.

"Me, too. It was great. And I really liked hearing you play."

"Thanks. Luckily, I play a lot better than I bowl. So, what are you up to?"

"I just had my first driving lesson. Aunt Karen took me out in the truck."

"Cool! How did it go?"

"Let's see . . . I almost killed a cow, then I almost killed my aunt."

"Really? Around here, they call that thinning the herd."

"Well, sign me up, then," I said. We laughed.

"So, you ready for our second date?"

This girl didn't waste any time.

"I think I can handle it. What do you have in mind?"

"I want to show you around Madison. It may not be San Francisco, but it's an awesome little city and very hip. How about tomorrow?"

"Sounds great," I said.

"My mom will drive us. Far as I know, she's never hit a cow."

❉

The next day, Laura's mom dropped us off at the University of Wisconsin, right in the middle of Madison. Mrs. Kearns had some business in the city, so Laura and I would be on our own until the evening.

Overlooking Lake Mendota, the university was beautiful and everything was in the full bloom of summer. There must have been 50 sailboats on the water, each with its own colorful sails. The campus was bustling with kids starting the summer session. Students tossed Frisbees and footballs around, while others, half-naked, sunned themselves on the lawns.

"This place is amazing," I said, not knowing where to look next.

"Yeah, it's a great school. I've played here several times."

Laura showed me around the campus, starting with the massive library. Then we saw the gym where Wisconsin played their Big Ten basketball games. She stopped by the music department, where she was a minor celebrity. Some students and even professors came over to greet her. She seemed a little embarrassed by all the attention.

"Didn't know you were such a rock star," I said.

"Yeah, right. I play classical piano. That doesn't make me a rock star; it makes me a music geek."

One of the neatest things about the university was that it had its own homemade ice cream, made right on campus from their own homegrown cows. People come from all over the Midwest just to try it. We ordered sundaes and took them outside to a spot overlooking the lake.

"If this is what college is like, bring it on—I'm ready," I said. "You think you might go here?"

"Nah, too close to home. I'm thinking of going to Juilliard in New York. It's probably the best music school in the country. I'd have to audition, and they only take like one out of a hundred who try out."

"Yeah, like you'll ever have to sweat it." The girl was only 16, and she already had a future. Me? The only thing I knew for sure about *my* future was that I had a dentist appointment sometime in August.

"What about you, Andy? Where do you want to go to college?"

"Honestly? I haven't thought about it much. I'm kind of interested in journalism, and I've heard Northwestern is good."

"Northwestern is really good. So you're going to be a writer, huh?"

"I don't know. It changes every week. It's, like, there's nothing out there, career-wise, that I'm really dying to do. It must be hard for you to relate to that. You're lucky."

"Why?"

"Well . . . uh. . . . " I'm such an idiot. I've just called a girl in a wheelchair lucky. Sometimes I wish my mouth came with a mute button. Or at least a very large sock I could stuff in it. I tensed up a bit and tried to make myself clear.

"What I mean is you have this amazing gift. You know you're gonna do *something* with it. You've got like a zillion possibilities. That's more than almost anyone else our age has right now."

"Gee, thanks, I guess." Laura said, not looking too optimistic. "I know what you mean, Andy, and I am lucky, believe me, I know it. It's just not exactly all that simple and mapped out, you know?"

I felt bad for making it sound like she had some kind of free pass.

"I mean, I still want to go to college, get an education, experience living away from home and all."

"Yeah. I can't wait to get out of the house," I said.

"It is a little scary, though. Leaving my mom, living alone. But it'll be totally cool to have my own place someday."

Laura looked out on the lake, deep in thought. There was so much going on behind those beautiful green eyes. She was a thinker, and I liked that. I'd always thought of myself as a thinker, but I was an amateur compared to her.

"Come on, let me show you around town," Laura said, leading the way. We crossed a couple of streets and were soon in the middle of a real college town. The main drag was lined with fast-food places, record stores, coffeehouses, bookstores, and bars—lots of bars.

"This is my favorite record store in the whole world," Laura said, as she rolled into Spin City. The place was packed mostly with college students, but there were also some teenagers like us.

The aisles were narrow, and Laura had to carefully maneuver around the customers. But this was easy compared to reaching the CDs. You had to be standing to search them.

Laura handled this by pulling her chair up as close as she could get it to the shelves, then sliding herself onto the edge of her seat so she could reach up as far as she could stretch. There were still a lot of CDs she couldn't get to, and it gave me a glimpse of what she had to go through every day. But it didn't even faze her.

"Have you ever heard Jenny Lewis?" she asked.

"No. Sounds like chick music."

"*Chick* music? I see. So what does a macho guy like you listen to?" This was a shot, and I probably deserved it.

"Different things. A little rap. . . . I like Arcade Fire, but I also like the Beatles."

"The Beatles, thank God. I thought I was going to have to ditch you right here."

"Hey, give me a break. Music is a personal thing."

"I know, I'm just messing with you. But you really should keep an open mind, you know, try different sounds. Follow me," Laura said, whipping her chair around and heading down the aisle. We left the Rock/Pop section and headed toward the back of the store, where there were hardly any customers.

"Don't tell me. This is the Classical section," I said. "I can tell by how empty it is."

"That's cold. True, but cold," Laura said. She stopped at a particular bin and started to rifle through the CDs. "Here. I'm going to personally recommend a classical artist I think you can get into." She handed me the CD.

"Whoa, this is you! You have your own record?" I said it way too loud, and several people up the aisle turned and stared at us. Laura was on the cover, sitting at the piano in a fancy dress. LAURA KEARNS: PIANO CONCERTOS.

"That is so cool," I said, this time keeping my voice down.

"Thanks. It's my first record. There's another one coming out in November."

"Well, I'm definitely buying this one," I said.

"Andy, you don't have to do that, I can give you one. . . . "

"No, I really want to buy it, but you have to autograph it for me."

"You got it. And I think I make, like, 13 cents on each one. Can you buy another 10?" We laughed.

At the checkout counter, I handed the clerk the CD, and then I pointed at Laura. "That's her," I said proudly.

The clerk looked at the CD, then at Laura, then back at the CD. A smile spread across his face. "You still gotta pay for this," he said.

When we got outside, Laura reached into her backpack and pulled out a felt-tip pen. I unwrapped the CD and handed it to her, then watched as she scribbled. Then she handed it back to me with a big smile. *To Andy: My new friend, who I hope will become an old friend. May music always be in your heart. Laura*

"That's really nice. Thank you," I said. "I wonder

what I can get for this on eBay." Laura smacked me and rolled away down the street.

"Come on," she said. "I have to buy my mom a birthday present."

We crossed the main street and walked a few blocks to a large, three-story department store. It was like a small Macy's, only a lot hipper. You could tell because the mannequins in the window had tattoos. There was a revolving door that most people were using, but there was no way Laura's chair could navigate that. Instead, Laura rolled on for another half block to the wider automatic doors. Once inside, she headed right for the elevators.

"Mom's birthday is next Tuesday, so I'd better start looking. Are you cool with that?"

"Sure, no problem." I didn't have the heart to tell her that I *hate* shopping and that my time limit in a department store is all of about 90 seconds. We went up to the third floor, to the women's clothing department. I was the only guy up there, with the exception of an overeager salesperson, who immediately pounced on us.

"What can I help you with?" he asked, way too enthusiastically.

"We're just looking, thanks," Laura said. The guy walked away, disappointed. She went over to a rack and started looking, checking every single item. Standing there, I realized that this was going to take a lot longer than my standard 90 seconds.

"Now *this* is cute, isn't it, Andy?" She held up a frilly lavender thing—I guessed it was a blouse.

"I guess." What did I know?

Laura took the frilly thing off the hanger and held it up. "Andy, how tall are you?" This couldn't be good.

"Five-seven," I said.

"Close enough. Mom's five-six. Could you be a pal and model this for me?"

"Did I say five-seven? I'm actually six-three. I just have really bad posture." She laughed.

"You want me to try this on?"

"No, silly. Just hold it up in front of yourself. Unless you *want* to put it on."

"Watch it," I said. Okay, why not? I could be a pal. I took the blouse and held it up to my chest, then struck a model's pose.

"It's adorable," Laura said.

"And it's his color." It was the salesman, who'd materialized out of nowhere.

"It's not for me, it's for her mom," I said, irritated.

"Thanks, Andy. That was sweet."

"You're welcome. But I draw the line at underwear."

Laura laughed. "That's good to know." Laura handed the blouse to the sales guy to ring up. After we completed that transaction, we headed toward the elevators. There, Laura stopped to look at the two female mannequins. Each was decked out in a stark white tennis outfit, with matching shoes, shorts, and sweater. Each wore a colorful baseball cap, and each held a tennis racquet. Laura smiled as she surveyed the display.

"What?" I asked.

She got this mischievous look in her eye as she grabbed a white tennis sweater from the stack and quickly pulled it on over her T-shirt. Then she put on a baseball cap and took a tennis racquet from one of the mannequins, positioning her chair right beside her. With the racquet in her hand as if she were returning a serve, Laura froze in place. She'd turned herself into a third mannequin. She didn't even blink.

"Nice," I said. "When your music career dries up, you'll have something else to fall back on."

Soon, two middle-aged women wandered toward us.

"This should be good," Laura said out of the corner of her mouth.

I hid behind a clothes rack, giving Laura center stage. She stayed absolutely still and was just another mannequin—one that just happened to be in a wheelchair. The women stopped about 10 feet away.

"Don't you just love those outfits?" the first woman said.

"Exquisite," replied the second one. "And look at that—a disabled mannequin. I've never seen that before."

"And she looks so real."

I had to bite my lip to keep from losing it. Laura was incredible, not moving a muscle. As the two turned to walk away, Laura sneezed loudly. The women froze in their tracks and slowly turned around. Then Laura swung her racquet, and both women screamed. They ran down the aisle as if the building were on fire.

"It's not disabled," Laura called out after them. "It's *physically challenged!*" I ran over to her, laughing all the way.

"That was brilliant," I said.

"Did you see how white they turned?"

"You're crazy, you know that?" I said.

"It's not crazy, it's *mentally challenged!*" We both laughed. I'd never met anyone like her before. She was smart, very funny, a little wild, and more than a little nuts. She was so much fun to be with.

Laura put the cap and tennis racquet back, and we took the elevator down to the first floor.

"You hungry?" she asked.

"I'm, like, always hungry."

"Good. There's this great pizza place up the street."

As we hit the automatic doors, a loud screeching alarm went off. People turned and stared at us, and before we knew it, a burly guy in a gray security uniform ran up to Laura.

"Excuse me, miss. I believe you're leaving with our sweater."

"Oh wow!" Laura said, looking down at the white tennis sweater she'd forgotten to take off. "I tried this on and forgot all about it."

"Right. Like I haven't heard that one before."

The security guy took the handles of Laura's wheelchair and pulled her back into the store.

"What do you think you're doing?" Laura said.

"You'll have to come with me, miss."

"Hold on, mister," I said. "She wasn't stealing the sweater. She honestly forgot she had it on."

The guy didn't even look at me. He asked, "What's your name, miss?"

"Jane. Jane Austen," Laura said, as I tried to keep a straight face.

"Miss Austen, we have you on our security tape putting the sweater on in the middle of the store."

"Get real," Laura said. "Why would I want a lame tennis sweater? Do I look like I can play tennis?"

The guy turned red as he searched for an answer.

"I don't know, Miss Austen, I'm just doing my job."

"So, your job is to harass the handicapped?" Laura said.

"Don't you mean the *physically challenged,* Jane?" I asked. Laura stifled a laugh as the security guy stood there, clueless.

"Look, just give me back our sweater, and we'll forget this ever happened," he replied.

Laura pulled the sweater off over her head and tossed it at him. We turned around and headed for the door.

"Sorry for the misunderstanding, Miss Austen. And I've read all your books." Laura and I stopped in our tracks and turned back to the security guy. He was smiling from ear to ear, pointing at us as if to say "Gotcha!"

"That was wild," I said, as we hit the sidewalk.

"Totally. We got the only rent-a-cop in Wisconsin who's read Jane Austen."

"That was definitely the most fun I ever had shopping," I said.

"Well, you've obviously been shopping with the wrong people," Laura said, smiling.

After that, we ate some pizza and tooled around Madison. We even visited the state capitol building. Madison was very cool, just like Laura'd said, but it really didn't matter where I was. It was all about who I was with.

15
Suicide Rock

"Dude, your *second* date! This is getting serious," Brad said in that annoying way of his. We were sitting up in our beds the next morning, and he was pumping me for the play-by-play details of my day in Madison with Laura.

"So?"

"So nothing, Brad. It was a lot of fun. Madison's a very cool place, and Laura is . . . amazing." I couldn't suppress a smile.

"Whoa, you've got it bad, bro," Brad said.

"I do not have it bad, you tool," I said, but the second I'd said it, I wondered. Laura was leaving that morning for Chicago, where she was going to perform at Northwestern University. She'd be gone overnight, and I actually felt myself missing her already. Maybe I did have it bad, whatever "it" was.

"Hey," Brad said, "a few of the kids are going hiking and swimming at Fortune Lake today. You want to come along?"

"Me? You're inviting me hang with you and your

129

friends? Who are you, and what have you done with my brother?"

"Very funny. But don't get all pissy. If you don't want to go, fine. But it's gonna be fun. We'll hike up to this place called Suicide Rock, then down to this amazing lake with waterfalls and stuff."

"Sounds cool," I said, still wondering why Brad was inviting me into his world.

❖

An hour later, I was sitting in the very rear seat of a Ford Explorer with Brad and his new friends. They were a chatty bunch, although no one seemed to want to chat with me.

A tall, skinny kid named Curt was driving, and his girlfriend Erin sat with him in front. Brad was in the back with a cute girl named Claire, who played with her hair and seemed more interested in Brad than he was in her. I kept my mouth shut and stared at the back of their heads, wondering what I was doing there.

Most of the conversation centered on music, until Claire asked Brad about California. Having never been there, the other kids had this fantasy that everyone in California lived on a surfboard.

Brad didn't let them down, making San Francisco sound like an ocean paradise and making himself sound like the king of the surfers. He somehow forgot to mention that he didn't even own a surfboard and hadn't been near the beach in about two years. My brother the bullshitter strikes again.

I got my first look at Suicide Rock as we drove into the parking area of Fortune Lake. I must say it lived up to its name, looking like the perfect place to end it all. It wasn't just high; it was steep. And it had big jagged boulders stacked on top of one another. My heart beat faster just looking at it.

"So, how did it get the name Suicide Rock?" I asked.

"Thirty-seven people bought it on this rock," Claire said, casually. "They either jumped or accidentally fell."

I was *so* hoping that this was an exaggeration—by, like, 37.

"Looks tougher than it is," Curt said. "I've climbed this sucker, like, 50 times, so follow me, and I'll get you up there the easiest way."

"Dude, the view at the top is awesome," Erin added.

We slipped our backpacks on and headed for the rock.

"I can do this," I told myself. "Just keep up, that's all."

Curt led the way, starting up a well-worn trail. The girls followed, and Brad and I were behind them. The first hundred yards or so were easy, and we almost jogged up the hill. The pack on my back was light, but it was bouncing around. When the water bottle in the pack kept thumping me in the same spot between my shoulder blades, I stopped for a second to reposition it, then double-timed to catch up.

Without much warning, the climb started getting steeper. The easy trail gave way to a difficult stairway of rocks and boulders. With each new rock, you had to find a foothold, a ledge, or a crack to plant your feet, and you hoped it wasn't a slippery one. Then you had to pull yourself up by your hands onto the rock above.

It took strength and balance, and I was really proud to be keeping up with Brad. Then it dawned on me: he was going slower for my sake. Okay, it might have been nice of him, but it still pissed me off a little.

Curt and the girls were excellent climbers, and they were getting way ahead of us up the rock.

"Hey, guys!" Curt shouted down to us. "When you reach the big red boulder, go up the *left* side. The rocks are loose on the right."

"Gotcha," Brad shouted back.

We were only about a third of the way up the rock, but we were already high enough to have a great view of the lake below. I started breathing harder and was sweating a lot. Then I turned a corner and came to a narrow ridge with a nasty drop on the other side. If you lost your balance here and slipped, it was going to be ugly.

I looked down for just a second and wished I hadn't. The sheer height of the cliff stopped me right in my tracks.

I told myself to slow down and move more carefully. There were footholds in every rock; you just had to find them. I carefully climbed up one big boulder and then another, making decent progress. I was getting pretty good at this. That's when I planted my foot on a small rock that gave way. I slid down about 10 feet, scraping my arm the whole way. But luckily, I'd landed on my feet.

No big deal—a little blood, a little less skin, but it was only a minor setback. I decided to take a little break and catch my breath. When I looked around, I realized that I was now ahead of Brad by about a hundred feet. When did that happen? *How* did that happen?

As Brad started closing the gap between us, I could see that he was sweating heavily and breathing kind of hard—much more than I was.

"You alright, Brad?"

"Yeah."

"You sure?"

"I don't know, Andy."

"What's the matter?"

"I'm not alright, okay?"

This didn't sound like my brother. And as he came closer, I could see that his legs were shaking.

"Brad, what's wrong?"

"Andy, I can't do this," he said in a breathless whisper.

"What do you mean?"

"I'm afraid of heights."

"You're afraid of heights?" I shouted.

"Thank you for telling all of Wisconsin."

"You just realized this?"

"I don't know. I guess. I mean, I haven't been up this high since . . . since ever."

"Okay," I said. "Just relax, take a deep breath, and don't look down."

"I'm not looking down. I can't even look up. Don't you see? I can't *do* this. If I go any higher, I just know I'm gonna fall off these rocks and die. Damn, why did I do this? Andy, I'm scared."

Brad was shaking hard—really trembling. His eyes started welling up. I'd never seen him like this. This wasn't *my* brother. *My* brother was the jock who never had a problem with any kind of physical stuff. He wasn't just confident, he was cocky. And he was *never* scared.

133

And here I thought he'd been hanging back for my sake. But no. Brad had been in trouble from the start. So *that's* why he'd wanted me to come along. If he got into trouble, I was someone he could turn to. The thing was, I had no idea what to do. I put a hand on his shoulder and could feel him still shaking.

"Come on, slowpokes," Claire called from above. "Get your butts up here. You can see the whole lake!"

Brad looked up, and then he looked at me. He wasn't just scared. He was embarrassed, and heading toward humiliated.

"Guys. What are you doing down there, making a sandwich?" It was Curt, who was now on his way down to us.

"Great," Brad said quietly to me, swallowing hard. "I'm such a wuss."

We just stood there in silence. Brad couldn't look at me, and I had no idea what to say. Then we had company. Curt had bounded down the rock like some kind of mountain goat.

"Could you guys be any slower? What's going on?"

Curt looked at Brad, then at me. Brad looked back blankly. He was going to lose it any second.

I had to think fast. I blurted, "I'm scared, Curt. I'm afraid of heights."

Brad turned to me with this stunned look. I wasn't totally sure he was picking up on what I was doing, so I looked him right in the eye this time.

"Brad, you said you'd take me down. I want to go down, now!" I might have poured it on a little thick, but at least Curt bought it.

"Okay, Andy, I'll take you down," Brad said calmly. I'll never forget the look of relief on his face.

"What'd you bring him for, anyway?" Curt asked, looking at me like I was some kind of freak.

"Sorry," Brad said. "You guys go on ahead. We'll just hang down there 'til you're ready to go."

"Whatever," Curt said in disgust. Then he turned to me. "Next time stay home, you wuss." He shook his head and started climbing back up the rock.

Brad was staring at his shoes. Finally, he looked up at me. His eyes were red, and I could hear the tightness in his throat.

"You okay?" I asked.

"Yeah."

"Maybe we better start down."

"Okay."

"You want to hold on to me?"

He didn't answer. He just kept looking at me. "Bro, I can't believe you did that."

"Hey, it's no big deal."

Brad smiled ever so slightly, looking at me in a way I'd never seen before. Now *I* was getting choked up, so to avoid a very awkward moment, I turned and started down the rock.

"Andy."

I stopped and turned back toward him. "Yeah?"

"It *was* a big deal. A very big deal. Thanks."

"Forget it," I said, knowing neither of us ever would.

So my brother followed me down Suicide Rock. We went slowly and carefully, and he held on to me several times.

For the first time ever in my life, Brad actually needed me. And I was glad to be there for him.

I wouldn't realize it right away, but things would be different between us after that day at Suicide Rock.

16

One Smart Pig and Three Idiot Humans

"Push, Andy—you're not pushing!" Aunt Karen shouted.

"I'm pushing as hard as I can. I'm just not used to having my hands on a pig's butt, okay?"

"Think of it as a growth experience," she said.

"In another minute, it's gonna be a *barfing* experience."

We were trying to get Margaret into the pickup truck— all 230 pounds of her. And Margaret did *not* want to go. She was squealing loudly, her way of laughing in our faces. Then Uncle Jim came to our rescue.

"Do you realize you're being outsmarted by a pig?" he said.

"Very funny, Jim. You got any better ideas?" Aunt Karen said.

Uncle Jim took an apple out of his pocket, held it in front of Margaret's nose, and then threw it into the truck. Margaret instantly ran in after it and now was safely in the truck. Uncle Jim quickly put up the tailgate, then turned to us with a satisfied smile.

"Big deal," Aunt Karen said. "Anybody can do it using food as bait."

Minutes later, we were on our way to the Oshkosh County Fair. Laura was meeting me there, and I couldn't wait to see her.

She'd called me when she returned from Chicago, and we talked for over an hour. I told her about Suicide Rock and the incident with Brad. She said what I did was heroic, and although I laughed at this, it was nice to hear it, coming from her. I'd mentioned how Brad already seemed like a different person, starting at breakfast, when—a first—he actually gave me the last piece of bacon.

The Oshkosh County Fair was one of the largest in Wisconsin, and it lasted for most of the summer. There were rides, a midway with carnival games, contests, tons of food, live music, and lots of animals. The local 4-H clubs held various competitions for cows, horses, sheep, pigs, and anything else that smelled bad and had four legs.

"So there's really a beauty contest for pigs?" I asked.

"Of course. Pigs can be beautiful, too," Aunt Karen said. "If you must know, they judge pigs on grooming, response to commands, and stature. Margaret has a real shot in the 300-pounds-and-under division."

"I can't wait for the swimsuit competition," Uncle Jim said. Aunt Karen didn't quite see the humor in this and smacked him on the arm.

We were now in downtown Oshkosh, and Uncle Jim stopped at a busy intersection. Just as he started across, a car ran the light from the other side, and he had to slam hard on the brakes. "You idiot!" he yelled.

"Relax, Jim, everyone's fine."

"Not exactly." Uncle Jim was looking in his rearview mirror. "I think we just lost our beauty queen."

"What?" Aunt Karen screamed.

Stopping short had thrown open the truck's tailgate, and Margaret had bounced out of the truck, right onto Central Boulevard.

"Pull over, Jim—now!"

"I'm trying to, but I'd like to not get us all killed in the process."

Uncle Jim steered the truck to the curb, then we all jumped out. Margaret was waddling across the street while angry drivers honked and swerved to avoid her. Margaret looked as surprised to see the cars as the drivers were to see her. It was all too much for me, and I busted up laughing.

"This isn't the least bit funny, mister," Aunt Karen snapped. "Come on. Let's go get her!" Aunt Karen waddled off into traffic, not quite as gracefully as Margaret. Uncle Jim took off, and I followed. For the record, neither of us waddled.

Now, there's something you have to understand about pigs. They may waddle, but they're really a lot faster than they look, especially when people are honking at them and screaming four-letter words.

Fueled by pure fear, Margaret quickly made her way up to the sidewalk, through a parking lot, and right through the automatic doors into the Oshkosh Mall as we all ran in after her. We heard the screams immediately.

Startled shoppers ran and dove out of the way as this wild-eyed pig slipped and slid on the newly polished mall floor. One poor kid tossed his corn dog 20 feet in the air.

With her hooves scraping across the floor, Margaret skidded past the Gap and Hold Everything, then finally came to a stop when she reached Cheese World. The overwhelming, pig-stopping odor of more than 500 cheeses must have appealed to her somehow, because she wandered in and sniffed her way around the Goudas and cheddars.

Uncle Jim ran into the store and tried to coax Margaret out. "Time to leave, Margaret. Come on, girl."

Margaret snorted something back that sounded insulting. Uncle Jim then tried to grab her by the neck, but she bucked her head and knocked him into the Limburger display.

That's when the pig turned and headed out the door, right to where I was standing.

"Grab her, Andy!" Aunt Karen shouted, at last arriving on the scene, all out of breath.

Never having caught a moving pig before, I wasn't exactly sure how to go about this. But I didn't have much time to think about it. As Margaret ran past me, I dove and wrapped my arms around her. The next thing I knew, I was being dragged through the mall on my stomach as startled people looked on.

"Hang on, Andy, stay with her," Aunt Karen shouted.

Easy for her to say. There was no way to keep any kind of grip on this pig's prickly hide, and soon I was desperately grabbing her squiggly tail. This really pissed Margaret off, making her shake her big butt 'til she tossed me off like a piece of lint.

People came over to help me up. Although I was only a little scraped up, I was very embarrassed. Aunt Karen ran over, panting. "Nice try, kid," she said, "but you've got no future in the rodeo."

Now Margaret was trotting even faster than before, passing the Pretzel Palace and the Sunglass Shack, heading straight for Victoria's Secret. I followed her, arriving just in time to hear the screams of two underwear-clad women who were sprinting out of the fitting room. I recognized the purple lace panties from page 37 of my mom's latest catalogue.

Meanwhile, the pig made her way into a dressing room and at last plopped herself down on the floor, exhausted from all the excitement. Then she began munching on a fleeing customer's leather purse.

Uncle Jim raced in, trailed by a red-faced Aunt Karen.

"There you are, Margaret. You naughty, naughty girl!" she scolded. The store manager came up to her, looking very pale.

"What the devil is this pig doing in my store?"

"Shopping," Aunt Karen replied, not skipping a beat. Then she cautiously approached Margaret's cubicle and spoke calmly to the pig. "Margaret, it's time to go. Now, we can do this the easy way, or we can do this the hard way. It's entirely up to you."

Margaret stood up and snorted in reply.

"Fine, be that way," Aunt Karen sighed. Then she pulled a tranquilizer gun from her purse, and Margaret snorted louder. Aunt Karen and Uncle Jim nodded to each other, then both sprang into action. The next few seconds were a blur, and I instinctively got out of the way.

First, Uncle Jim grabbed the pig and held her by her hind legs. Margaret squealed loudly and bucked, dragging him across the floor. Then Aunt Karen pulled the trigger and scored a direct hit.

Unfortunately, it was a direct hit on Uncle Jim instead of the pig! "Aghhh!" Uncle Jim cried out.

"Dammit, Jim! You're not the pig."

Just as Margaret was making a break for it, Aunt Karen fired again, hitting the pig in her side. Then she shot once more for good measure.

A grown man and a pig were now both out cold on the floor. And the Victoria's Secret manager looked like she was about to join them any second.

Now *this* was way more exciting than anything I'd ever seen in their catalogue!

※

Fifteen minutes later, we were all riding on a maintenance cart. With the head of mall security at the wheel, Aunt Karen and I propped up an unconscious Uncle Jim between us. Margaret rode in the back, passed out with her legs in the air, held down by bungee cords.

As we rode out of the mall, people stopped dead in their tracks and stared. When we finally got to the truck, six men helped us load the pig in back. Uncle Jim woke up, but he still wasn't quite himself.

"Where am I? What happened?" He looked groggily at Aunt Karen, wearing a dopey grin.

"You're fine, Jim. I shot you with a tranquilizer dart," Aunt Karen said.

"Why'd you do that?"

"It was an accident. I was trying to shoot the pig."

"And you couldn't tell the difference between us?"

"I . . . uh . . . you were both rolling around on the floor. It was total chaos. I took aim, and I missed. It was an accident, Jim."

Jim looked at her skeptically. "I wish I could believe that."

When I heard that, I started laughing. Then Aunt Karen aimed the tranquilizer gun at me.

That's when I stopped laughing.

17

One Crazy Night

We finally arrived at the fair, almost an hour late. Uncle Jim and Margaret were now wide awake, and the pig looked really pissed. Aunt Karen and Uncle Jim hurried Margaret over to the 4-H contest, and I went to meet Laura at the information booth. Her mom had dropped her off, and she'd been waiting for me all this time.

"Where were you, Andy?" Laura asked. "I was getting kind of worried." But she still managed a smile.

"I tried to call you, but my cell doesn't get good service here. And I'm late because I was chasing a pig through the Oshkosh Mall."

"Yeah, right. You probably use that one on all the girls you stand up."

"I *so* wish I were making this up." I told her the whole story, cracking her up, and making her sorry she missed it.

Despite my delay, Laura and I picked up right where we'd left off. We were getting more comfortable with each other by the minute.

Our first stop was the 4-H show grounds, to watch Margaret compete in her beauty contest. We got there just in time for her big debut in the 300-pounds-and-under division.

The contestants were walked up to the viewing platform and turned so the judges could see their best side. But if you ask me, a pig doesn't really have a best side.

The announcer was as serious as if he were at the Miss America Pageant: "Our next contestant is from Willowbrook Farms. Please give a nice welcome to the lovely Margaret!"

Laura and I applauded loudly as Aunt Karen led Margaret onto the viewing platform.

The pig had a rope around her neck—this would never happen to Miss New Jersey. Of course, Miss New Jersey probably wouldn't snort and pee right on the stage, which is what Margaret promptly did. Laughter erupted from several hundred spectators, who obviously didn't get out much.

Aunt Karen gritted her teeth and tried to laugh it off. "No more iced tea for you, little piggy."

But the damage was done, and things only got worse from there. Aunt Karen tried to turn Margaret around for the judges, but she refused to budge. Then, as the judges furiously scribbled on their score sheets, Margaret plopped down on the platform and fell asleep—those tranquilizer darts were still affecting the poor pig.

The crowd howled, and Aunt Karen's face turned many shades of red. At first, I actually felt sorry for her, but in the end, she got the last laugh as she bent down to scold the snoring pig: "That's it for you, sister. You're bacon, get it? You're gonna be tomorrow's breakfast!" She stormed off the stage, leaving the sleeping Margaret behind.

"Speaking of bacon," Laura said, "I'm starved."

If there was one thing the Oshkosh County Fair had plenty of, it was food. There were over 200 food stands serving everything from bratwurst to sushi. There were homemade pies, chili, barbecue, six kinds of cotton candy, and, of course, cheese.

Cheese was served on and with everything. I half expected them to have cheese-flavored cotton candy. But that was the one item I didn't have to sample.

Laura and I hit one of the barbecue shacks and pigged out on spareribs, coleslaw, and corn on the cob. The food was delicious, and we topped it off with Ma Carter's homemade apple pie—the blue ribbon winner in the fruit pie division.

Then we watched a pie-eating contest, where contestants had to eat as many pies as they could without using their hands. Some tight end from the University of Wisconsin won by eating 11 pies. He was fine, but I felt a little queasy.

"I'm never eating pie again," I said.

"Yeah, that wasn't pretty," Laura said. "What do you say we go check out the games on the midway?"

For the next couple of hours, we played every stupid carnival game they offered. It would've been boring with anyone else, but with Laura, it was a whole new level of fun. There was almost nothing she couldn't do.

We threw darts at balloons, softballs at milk bottles, and Ping-Pong balls into goldfish bowls. People would stop and stare occasionally, but Laura didn't seem fazed. She even won a stuffed panda bear that she named after me.

But there was one awkward moment, when we passed one of the music stages where people were dancing. Laura stopped and watched for a minute, and then rolled on without saying a word. I was never big on dancing, but I did wonder what it would be like to dance with her.

The sun was going down, casting a pretty orange glow that lit up the entire fair. I looked at Laura, who had this playful look in her eye, similar to the one she'd had in the department store when she pulled the mannequin stunt.

"There's one more game we have to play," she said.

At the far end of the midway was a horse race game. You had to shoot a squirt gun at plastic targets, and every time you hit one, your horse would move around the track toward the finish line. The booth was completely deserted, so Laura and I got to face off against each other.

"I'll take Citation," she said, positioning her wheelchair behind the corresponding squirt gun.

"Okay, I've got Man o' War."

"Typical macho choice," she said.

"Really," I said. "It's better than Citation. That's a traffic ticket."

"You're going down, Man o' War. You're horse meat."

"Oh yeah? We'll see, Traffic Ticket."

The guy manning the booth woke up from his nap and took our tickets. Then he flipped the switch to start the game.

"And they're off!" A voice bellowed.

As fast as we could, Laura and I squeezed the triggers of our squirt guns. Our horses were running neck and neck, and then we looked at each other.

"Your finger's getting tired, Andy. Give it up."

"In your dreams."

"It's Citation by a neck. Now Man o' War takes the lead," the computerized announcer said.

My eyes were like lasers on the target, and I fired as fast as I could. Then, without any warning, Laura turned her squirt gun on me, zapping me with hard streams of water.

"Aghh! Okay, you want to play rough?" I said.

I turned my gun on Laura and returned fire, blasting her right in the face. It was the ultimate squirt gun fight. We were only three feet apart, and getting really soaked. Laura was screaming and laughing. I was doing the same—minus the screaming.

"Hey, you two! What the hell do you think you're doing?" The guy in the booth was shouting, and Laura let go of the gun. She wheeled away from the booth, but I kept shooting at her until the guy turned off the water.

I ran after Laura and grabbed the wheelchair from behind, slowing her down to a stop. We both were still cracking up.

Laura's laugh was this funny, playful giggle, and that made me laugh even more. Her hair was wet, and she looked even hotter than usual.

"That's the most fun I've had in a long time," she said.

"Me, too! You *are* nuts, you know?"

"Yeah, I've heard that before."

Her stuffed panda was wedged into the chair at her side, as if it were sharing her seat. They looked kind of cute together.

"You feel like some cotton candy?" I asked. She nodded, grinning, and we headed to the food stands. We didn't speak for a while, both of us soaked and savoring the moment.

Four guys, high school age or maybe a bit older, appeared around the bend. They obviously had been drinking, and one could hardly walk. Loud and obnoxious, they shoved each other between huge burps. Laura saw them, looked at me, then rolled her chair out of their way.

One guy was chasing the drunkest kid, who was trying to elude him. As he looked over his shoulder at his pursuer, the drunk kid continued running at full speed—heading straight toward Laura.

I shouted out to warn him, but it all happened too fast. He crashed right into Laura, landing on her before falling off to the ground. Then Laura's panda fell into a muddy puddle of water.

"You asshole!" I yelled. "You could have really hurt her!"

I ran over to Laura, who looked shaken but undamaged. "You okay?" I asked. She nodded, but her bottom lip was quivering. Then the drunk got up and stared at Laura, smirking stupidly.

"Why don't you watch where you're going, jerk?" I snarled.

"Chill, kid. It's not like she actually can feel anything." He laughed, and so did his friends.

When I saw the look on Laura's face, the blood began rushing in my ears. Everything seemed to stop. Then, as if my right arm had a mind of its own, I swung and punched the drunken kid in the face. It was such a reflex reaction, I didn't know I was gonna hit him until I already had—and my hand started to hurt like crazy.

Then things happened very quickly. Time went into fast-forward. The kid went down in a heap, and I heard Laura scream. Out of the corner of my eye, I saw the blur of a hand—but a split second too late. One of the other guys had rushed me, and I met his flying fist with my eye.

I've heard that in the heat of battle, you don't feel pain because your adrenaline's pumping too much. But I'm proof that it's not true, since my eye hurt the instant that guy hit me. I fell backward on my butt from the punch, and three guys landed on top of me.

Laura was screaming again, and then I heard her yell "Help!"

Beneath the jumbled mass of elbows, knees, and fists, I kept rolling to somehow dodge the blows. But a guy can only roll so far, and the three older guys caught me and pinned me down. With blood running from his nose, the drunken guy I'd hit was now leaning over me. Both of his fists were cocked, and he looked absolutely insane. Now I was really scared.

That's when the strangest thing happened. Somehow, from out of nowhere, this big guy threw himself at the guy on top of me, knocking him off. Relieved of my attacker now, I could have gotten up, but I was too frozen by fear to move.

Then I was shocked to see that my rescuer was actually Brad. My brother had come to the fair with his friends and had heard Laura screaming. Brad didn't even realize who he'd saved at first, because when he looked down at me, he did a classic double take.

"Andy?" He was as astonished as I was.

Now the other three boys rushed Brad, but they didn't have a chance in hell. Brad punched one in the stomach, dropping him instantly to his knees. He clocked another guy in the jaw. Then the third kid, obviously the smartest, ran off. The two remaining jerks sat on the ground as Brad stood over them, seething.

"You bastards think you're tough, ganging up four against one?" The boys just stared at the ground, too scared to meet Brad's gaze. Then Brad dragged them to their feet, holding each one by the neck.

"Get out of here," he shouted. "And if you ever come anywhere near my brother again, you won't walk away next time."

The boys looked at each other. Then, as if on cue, they both took off.

As I stood up, Brad came over.

"You okay, Andy?"

"Yeah, but I don't know what would've happened if you hadn't showed up. Thanks for saving my butt, Brad."

"Hey, I owed you one, bro."

I bit my lower lip, then I looked around for Laura, who'd moved to the side and looked pale. I walked over and asked, "Are you okay?" She nodded silently.

"Laura, this is my brother, Brad, and Brad, this is Laura." Brad walked over and extended his hand. Laura took it with both of hers.

"Nice to meet you, Brad. I like your timing."

Brad laughed. "Yeah, well, I couldn't have done it without your screaming. What the hell happened here?"

I quickly told Brad the story, and he said he was proud of me. It meant a lot coming from him. He said he'd see me back home, then turned to walk away. I stopped him and gave him a hug. He clutched me really tight, and we exchanged a meaningful look. He nodded once, acknowledging that no other words were needed. For the first time in a long time, I was proud to have him as my brother.

Brad left, and Laura and I were alone. As I walked over to her, I touched a big welt over my eye. The right side of my head felt like it was being hit repeatedly with a hammer.

"You should get a snow cone," Laura said.

"I'm not really hungry right now."

"I mean for your eye, stupid."

There was an edge in her voice now that I hadn't heard before. She motioned for me to lean down. She ran a finger over my eyebrow with a look of concern that I've seen only from my mother.

"You could've been really hurt, Andy. Why the hell did you hit that guy?"

I really couldn't answer her. Why *had* I done it? Up to today, I'd lived my life as a practicing coward. Not only had I never been in a fight before, I usually ran the other way if one broke out. So why did I start a fight with four boys, all older and bigger than me?

"Andy," Laura said, snapping me out of my mini-trance and wanting an answer.

"I don't know. I guess I kind of snapped. I still can't

believe what that idiot said. I couldn't just stand there and let him get away with it."

"So you did it for me?"

"Well, yeah."

"Well, next time, *don't,* okay?"

"Don't worry, I won't," I said, raising my voice. Laura rolled away from me, and I walked after her.

"What exactly is your problem, anyway?"

"I don't have a problem. I just don't need you defending the *crippled girl.*"

Whoa. Defending the crippled girl. Is that what I'd been doing? Maybe it was. And would that be such a bad thing?

"I'm sorry," I said. "The guy was being an asshole, and I just reacted, okay? Hey, if I knew you were going to totally freak about it, I never would've bothered."

This time, I was the one who walked away. I went over to the nearest bench and sat down. This was all getting too weird. It was only our third date, and we were already having our first fight. I felt sick to my stomach and still wondered what I'd done wrong.

After a few minutes, it was Laura who came over to me.

"I'm sorry. I shouldn't have snapped at you."

"No big deal," I said, lying.

"Andy, it *was* a sweet thing you did, defending me. But it was stupid, okay? It wasn't worth almost getting your skull cracked. If you'd been seriously hurt, I would have felt totally responsible."

"Why? You didn't do anything. It was those assholes who started it all."

"I know, but if something worse had happened, it would've been all because of me. I don't expect you to understand. It's just that . . . oh, forget it."

"No, Laura, let's not forget it. What are you trying to say?"

Laura's face seemed to tense up as she looked away.

"I feel . . . I feel like enough of a burden already."

"You're not a burden. People are just stupid."

"You think that's breaking news to me? What happened tonight . . . do you think I've never heard it before? I'm used to it. I mean, as much as you ever get used to it."

She was right. I never would understand. There was no way that I could. But something on my face must have said "Try me," because Laura started opening up.

"It's funny. When you get your first chair, they send out this person who shows you how to get around in it—you know, how to go forward, backward, make turns, go uphill and downhill. They take, like, three days to show you everything you'll ever need to do in that chair. Everything—except how to deal with it.

"What they don't tell you is how the whole world looks down on you because now you're only three feet tall. You get used to that, too. But there's one thing you never quite get used to: the pity look. That's the look you get from almost everyone.

"I have a friend in a chair who described it perfectly. She said, 'Being in a chair, you become the poster child for how lucky everyone else is.'"

What could I possibly say to that? I just stood there in silence, trying very hard not to look down on her.

Laura shook her head. "I'm sorry, Andy."

"For what?" I asked.

"That was like, sooo not cool. I barely know you, and I'm bumming you out big time."

"I'm not bummed out at all."

"You're not? You don't think I'm some kind of drama queen?"

"No. I think you're amazing," I said.

"You do?" She actually started to blush.

"Oh, yeah."

She bit her lower lip, looking like she might cry. "You still feel like cotton candy?"

"No," I said, touching my aching eye. "But I'm about ready for that snow cone."

Laura smiled, and I felt the tightness in my chest relax. I picked up her stuffed panda bear from the puddle and wrung out all the water I could. I handed it to Laura, who held it close to her. I pushed her toward the food stands, and for once, she let me.

Neither of us spoke for a while, but it wasn't an awkward silence. Instead it was a welcome break. I needed some time to let the last 15 minutes sink in, and she probably did, too.

Laura had really opened up to me, and I was hoping she didn't regret it. I'd wanted to put my arms around her and tell her she could talk to me about anything. But I didn't have the courage—we were still so new to each other. Yet somehow I felt that I already knew her better than I knew any of my other friends.

❖

So there I sat, with a cherry snow cone against my eye. It hurt, but Laura promised that the ice would take down the swelling. She was picking apart a big tuft of cotton candy and somehow managing to look cool eating it. The fair was even more crowded now, and the cooler night air was filled with the sounds of laughter and the screams of the roller coaster riders.

"You know what I haven't done in, like, forever?" Laura asked. "Ride the Ferris wheel."

"I'm there."

We made our way to the Ferris wheel, where the line wasn't very long. Most people wanted the faster, wilder rides. But looking up, I could see this was no wimpy Ferris wheel. It was at least 10 stories high, with 15 separate cars, each topped with a steel cage. Some of the cars were turning completely upside down, and the riders inside were screaming, in either joy or terror.

Laura and I quickly reached the front of the line. The tattooed ride operator, a very muscular guy, easily lifted Laura out of her chair and carried her into the car. I got in and sat next to her, and he pulled a long seat belt across both our laps.

"Keep this tight at all times. One of you falls out, I get fired. Oh—if you really want to get dizzy, just pull this handle," he said, pointing to a metal lever coming out of the floor.

Soon the car jerked, and we left the ground behind.

Laura giggled, and the breeze caught her hair, tossing it in every direction. The Ferris wheel picked up speed, and our car rose to the top. Then, just as quickly, it headed back down again.

"Okay," Laura said, "enough wimpy stuff." She pulled the lever toward us, and we immediately started spinning around backward, all while circling the huge wheel. It was the strangest feeling I'd ever had, with everything a dizzy blur of lights and colors, ground and sky. Laura screamed with delight. I wasn't quite as thrilled.

"I feel like my stomach's in a blender," I groaned.

Laura laughed, but I wasn't joking. Then we heard clanging as all the change fell out of my pockets. It bounced off the metal floor, then flew out of the car.

"There goes my college savings," I shouted, as Laura laughed even harder. Thankfully, she let up on the lever, and now we just rocked as we went around. My stomach settled down, but I still was totally dizzy.

"That was great!" said all twelve Lauras.

"The best," I lied.

After going around a few more times, the Ferris wheel started to slow. The view from up high was incredible; you could see the entire fairground below, and the night was so clear you could see almost half the state.

"I haven't been on this ride since I was four," Laura said.

Four? That was the year of her car accident.

"Well, you never really outgrow the Ferris wheel," I said. In a way, this was true. Being up there brought back a flood of memories, and it was like I was six years old again. At least, that's how I felt until Laura grabbed my hand.

I squeezed her hand, and my heart started beating faster. So much for six years old. I was 15 and feeling every second of it. I looked over at her, and she beamed with that awesome smile. I didn't exactly know what to do next. The Ferris wheel was unloading riders now, and our car was stopped at the very top.

I had to say something to break the silence. "Ride's stopping."

"Guess so," Laura said.

Then it hit me like this lightning bolt of guilt. This girl was so open and honest with me that I owed her the truth. So I dove right in and started confessing: "Laura, I lied to you the other day. I'm not going into junior year. I'm going to be a sophomore. I'm 15, not 16. I just said that because I thought you might be older and think I was an immature geek. Turns out you *are* older, and I *am* an immature geek, but you're so great and so cool and so honest, I feel terrible that I didn't tell you the truth. I promise I'll never . . . "

"Andy. Shut up, will you please?" She was moving toward me, getting closer and closer. Her eyes closed, her head tilted, and then her lips were on mine. I was officially being kissed by an older woman.

I closed my eyes just as Laura put her arms around my neck. I put my arms around her, too, and she felt wonderful. Whatever perfume she was wearing should have been declared illegal. Mixed with the strong smell of cotton candy wafting up from below, it's something I won't ever forget.

Laura's lips were warm, wet, and a little chapped. Her tongue was warmer, wetter, and tasted like sugar. We explored each other's dental work for a while. But however long it lasted, it was my first real kiss and I never wanted it to end.

But we had to come up for air. Our car was almost on the ground, and Laura put her head on my shoulder. We held each other tight, neither of us saying a word.

18

My First Dead Guy

I woke up the next day around noon, after sleeping for 11 hours straight. The emotional highs and lows of the last night had taken their toll.

As I got out of bed, every inch of my body hurt. All that rolling around on the ground with guys pouncing on you, well, you really feel it the next day.

Then there was my eye. The throbbing sent me to the mirror, and what I saw wasn't pretty. My eye was swollen half shut, and it was already turning purple. But as awful as it looked, it still brought on a smile. I was Andy Crenshaw, Tough Guy. Yeah, right.

I walked gingerly into the kitchen, where Brad was eating cornflakes.

"Nice eye," he said.

"Yeah," I said. "Strange night." I put ice into a dish towel, held it against my eye, then leaned against the counter.

"You all right?" Brad asked.

"I'm fine . . . thanks to you. You were amazing, man, like some kind of superhero."

Brad laughed. "Thanks, bro. It was kinda bizarre. First, I heard this girl screaming so I ran over to find out why. All I saw were, like, four guys on top of this other guy, so I just automatically reacted. But then I saw that guy was *you*. And that's when I got scared."

"Scared? You fought off four guys. You saved my ass. I'll never be able to repay you, Brad."

"Hey, don't even think about *that*. When I realized it was you, I would've fought a hundred guys. You're my *brother*, man.

"Look, I know we argue and give each other shit, but when things get tight, we've got each other's back. Just like you were there for me on the hike. We're *brothers*."

"Brothers," I said, realizing for the first time ever what that really meant. Brad got up from the table and gave me a hug.

"Dude, you need a shower," he said.

"Now *that's* my real brother," I said, as we both laughed. I headed off to the shower, but then stopped in my tracks. I turned back with an urge to tell him something else—a detail I'd never have opened up to him about just a couple of days ago.

"I kissed her."

He broke into a big smile. "That's great." Then he shook his head.

"What?"

"Wasn't it, like, just yesterday that you were crawling around, pulling yourself up on my leg?"

"Looks like I'm *still* pulling myself up on your leg."

I had only two days left in Wisconsin, and I wanted to spend every minute of them with Laura. She invited me over to hang out at her house for the day and then have dinner. Laura lived only a mile away on a quiet tree-lined street in an older part of town. Brad dropped me off in Uncle Jim's pickup.

Laura's mom opened the door, took one look at me, and immediately looked concerned.

"Andy, are you all right? Laura told me what happened."

"I'm fine, Mrs. Kearns. It looks a lot worse than it actually is."

"I have the perfect thing for that bruise."

"That really isn't necessary . . . " But she'd already headed to the medicine chest. Laura rolled into the entrance, then looked up at my bruise.

"Ouch."

"You should see the other guy," I said.

She laughed and said, "I'm glad you're here."

"Yeah, me, too."

"I had a great time yesterday," Laura said, "except for about 15 minutes."

"Yeah. The other seven hours were awesome."

Even though neither of us mentioned it, we were both talking about the kiss. Funny how you can talk about something without actually spelling it out.

Laura's mom came into the room with a tube of something and a long Q-tip.

"Mom, please," Laura protested.

"No, Laura. I have to take care of that eye," Mrs. Kearns said. "This stuff is like magic, and it won't hurt a bit. Sit down, Andy."

I did what I was told, and Laura's mom gently applied the ointment, which tingled but didn't actually sting.

"Now, I'm going to give you this tube. Use it every day until the bruising's gone."

"In case you were wondering, Mom used to be a nurse," Laura said.

"Thanks, Mrs. Kearns," I said.

"Thank *you*, Andy." She put her hand on my shoulder. "I made some sandwiches for you guys. Help yourself when you get hungry." Mrs. Kearns smiled and walked out of the room. I took a quick look around and instantly took in the huge concert piano that dominated the living room.

"Wow. That's a beautiful piano—and it's really big."

"Yeah. We bought it three years ago. It's the same kind I use in concerts."

"Will you play something for me?" I asked.

"Okay, if you want me to."

Laura rolled to the piano bench. She lowered an armrest on her chair, then hoisted herself onto the piano bench, using only her arms. It took a great deal of effort, and she strained as she positioned herself.

Laura sat up straight, took a deep breath, and gently touched the keys. I couldn't identify the classical piece she played, but whatever it was, I liked it.

"I *know* you know that one," she said.

"Of course. It's the one in B minor by that dead guy."

"Close enough," she said, waving me over to join her on the piano bench.

"Here's one you know." She broke into a rendition of the Beatles' "Obla Di, Obla Da." Soon, I was singing along with her and we couldn't keep from laughing.

"You have a very good voice, Andy Crenshaw."

"Nah, you were carrying me the whole time. Play another one for me."

She started in on another song, but then her cell phone beeped, signaling an incoming text message. Laura picked up her phone and flipped it open.

"It's my friend Katie. She wants me to call her right away. It'll just be a minute."

"No problem," I said. "Go ahead."

Laura hit a number on speed dial. "Hi, Katie, what's up?" She paused to listen, then blurted, "Oh my God! Brian Thomas? I can't believe it!"

Laura's face contorted into a mask of disbelief and sorrow, and her bottom lip started to quiver.

"When? Oh, this is so horrible. No, no, thanks for . . . no, I'd have heard about it sooner than later." She hung up the phone and looked up at me with the saddest eyes I've ever seen.

"What's wrong?"

"This kid from school—Brian Thomas. He killed himself last night."

"Oh, my God. Were you close to him?"

"Not really, but he sat next to me in a couple of classes. We did some projects together, and his locker was next to mine. He always helped me get things on the top shelf. I don't know if I ever really thanked him for it, and now I can't 'cause he's . . . "

"I'm really sorry, Laura." I didn't know what else to say. I looked in her eyes, and then I took her hand. She leaned her head on my shoulder, fighting back the tears.

"I wonder how he did it." She stared into space for a few seconds. "I have to go see him—now."

"What?"

"He's at Bones's funeral home. I want to see Brian with my own eyes. Would you please come with me, Andy?"

Whoa. You want me to come with you to see a dead kid? I really wasn't ready for this, and I really didn't want to go. I didn't reply either way, so Laura pushed it, saying simply, "Please."

Maybe it was the way she said it or the way she looked at me. My heart melted, and I reluctantly said, "Okay."

"Thanks, Andy," was all she said.

❖

Laura stared silently out the window for the short ride to Bones's funeral home. Mrs. Kearns punctuated the silence with typical motherly comments: "Only 15 years old." "What a shame." "His poor parents."

I was getting more nervous by the minute. Yes, I wanted to be there for Laura and be a true friend. But I was totally creeped out about the whole thing.

I'd been to only one funeral in my life—I was eight

when my grandfather died. All I remember is a lot of religious stuff, a bunch of strangers crying, and a boatload of food afterward at our house.

Once we were at Bones's place, Laura's mom got out of the car to set up her wheelchair. Then Laura turned to face me from her front seat.

"I really appreciate you coming with me, Andy."

I nodded stoically as Aunt Karen's four-egg omelet began creeping back up my throat. Once Laura was in her chair, her mom gave her a big hug—like she was almost afraid to let go.

The place was dimly lit and eerie. It was also totally quiet. I guess the dead can't make much noise.

A heavy-set woman behind a reception desk was reading *People* magazine.

"Hi, Flo," Laura said, as she wheeled herself up to the desk.

"Hey, sweetie," Flo said. "You here to see Bones?"

"Well, actually, I'm here to see Brian Thomas."

"Oh." Flo's smile changed to a pained expression. "What a terrible shame."

"Flo, this is my friend Andy."

"Nice to meet you, Andy."

"Hi, Flo."

She picked up the phone and hit a button. "Bones, Laura's here. She wants to see the Thomas kid." Flo hung up, saying, "He wants you to go on back."

Laura took a deep breath. "Flo, do you know how it happened? How did Brian die?"

"He O.D.'ed. Got hold of his mom's sleeping pills."

Laura nodded, as if that somehow was a relief. Then she turned to me. "You don't have to come in with me, Andy. You can just wait here if you want."

It helped to hear her say it, but the look in her eyes told me I had to go in there with her. I couldn't wimp out on her now. And as scared as I was, I was also kind of curious. I wanted to know what a dead person looked like. And I wondered how I'd handle it.

My knees had started shaking, and I was glad I wasn't wearing shorts. "I'm right behind you," I said. She smiled sadly and took my hand. I noticed hers was trembling, and holding it made me feel better.

We passed a chapel and then went down a long corridor. It seemed like the lights were getting dimmer. Before this trip, my father had kept telling me to be open to trying new things. Well, here I was, walking toward my first dead guy. *Okay, Dad, this sure is a new experience. I should get extra credit for this one.*

I opened the door to The Room, and Laura wheeled herself in. I began to follow her, resisting a sudden urge to turn and run.

Walking into the room, the first thing that hit me was the smell. It was a strong, sour odor that crept into your nostrils and stayed; it must have been the embalming fluids that keep bodies looking okay for viewing.

The room was cold, at least 20 degrees colder than normal, and I shivered involuntarily.

Bones stood in the center of the room, hovering over a long stainless steel table lit by a bunch of intensely bright lights. He wore a surgical gown, a mask, and gloves, as if he were doing surgery. Bones used instruments, hoses, and different colored liquids in clear glass containers, all on a stainless steel tray.

Laura rolled up to the table, but I stayed a couple of feet behind her. I could see more than I wanted right from where I stood.

Brian looked very young. He was lying on his back, covered by a sheet from the waist down, and seemed like he could've been sleeping. Although his eyes were closed, he seemed to be smiling a tiny smile—almost like he was having some amusing dream. But I could see how absolutely white he was, with no color at all in his skin. That's when I realized . . . this is what dead looks like. It was something I didn't expect.

Bones put down an instrument and came over to greet Laura. "Hey, sweetpea," he said, kneeling to put his arms around her. That's when the floodgates opened, and Laura burst into tears. She sobbed so hard that she shook. I felt awful—and totally useless. I offered Laura my hand, and she squeezed it very hard. Bones went to get her a box of tissues.

"Seemed like a nice kid," Bones said.

Laura nodded and choked back another sob, but then she caught her breath and spoke: "He was always really nice to me. Once for my birthday, he made me a horn for my wheelchair. It was the stupidest and sweetest thing I ever saw." Then she was crying again.

"I hate my job on days like this," Bones said. "Forty-two years, and I'll never get used to kids dying. It ain't natural. But I gotta get back to work—he has to be ready for the viewing tomorrow, then the funeral's on Friday."

Laura stopped crying, and Bones went back to the table. He picked up a makeup brush and added some color to Brian's face. Having stopped shaking by now, I went in for a closer look. Bones meticulously applied different colors to different parts of Brian's face. It was like he was bringing him back to life with his brush.

Laura leaned closer to the table. "I know I never told you this, Brian, but thanks for being so nice to me. I'll never, ever forget you." She wiped away a tear, then turned to Bones, saying, "I never thought he'd be one to kill himself."

"You just never know, sweetpea. Even if you think you know somebody real good, you never know what's goin' on in their heart or their head." Then he turned to me. "You okay, kid?"

"Yeah, I'm fine," I said.

"Good. 'Cause when you walked in, I thought I was goin' to have to put some color on you, too."

Laura smiled for a second and turned to me. "Thanks for coming in with me, Andy."

I wanted to say "It's nothing," but that would have been a lie. Instead, I just nodded, watching Laura as she studied Brian's face. If she could have willed him back to life with her eyes, he'd have gotten up from that table and walked out the door.

We stayed a few more minutes. Then Laura said her final good-byes to Brian. Afterward, we went outside, and I was relieved to breathe some fresh air. I sat on a bench next to Laura. We were both kind of numb and sat there without a word for a while.

"He was *our age,* Andy," she said.

"I know. It's so . . . unreal that he's dead."

"I just know I'm going to be looking for him when we go back to school."

"I know." We sat in silence for a while.

"What do you think happens to us when we die?" I asked.

"I'm not sure," she said. "And I was actually dead for five minutes."

Did I hear that right? "What do you mean?" I asked.

"It happened right after the accident. I was unconscious, and the doctors told my mom I was, like, clinically dead for a while."

"Whoa!"

"Luckily, I woke up with all my vital organs working. But I can't tell you what those five minutes were like. I don't remember a bright light, and there were no angels and no great feeling of peace. It was just one big blank for me. I wonder if it's like that for Brian."

"I think about death sometimes," I said. "I mean, not every day, or even once a week. But sometimes in the middle of the night, I'll wonder what's it's like . . . to be dead. Then I think about who's really gonna miss me and how hard they'll cry. I even wonder what my parents would do with my room. You think that makes me weird?"

"No."

"I don't think I could ever do it, though," I said.

"Do what?"

"Kill myself. I'm too much of a chicken."

"No, you're not. Maybe you're just brave. I think suicide's the easy way out."

I'd never looked at it like that, but Laura made me look at a lot of things in a new way. The conversation was getting interesting, and I wasn't sure I should ask her, but there was something I wanted to know. And this seemed like the right time.

"Did you ever think about doing it? You know, after the accident, with everything you went through later?"

"No, I didn't. It all just made me want to live even more. Life really sucks sometimes, but when it comes down to it, to me, it's better than the alternative."

Yeah, it sure is. I took Laura's hand, and she looked into my eyes.

"Andy, tell me the truth. After tomorrow, do you think we'll ever see each other again?"

"Of course we will! Why wouldn't we?"

"I don't know. We'll be half a country apart. Life is weird sometimes, and you really can't count on anything."

"I know what you mean. But it's not like we live on different planets. I'll get to you somehow, even if I have to walk."

She laughed and then said, "I'm really going to miss you, Andy."

"I'm going to miss you like crazy," I said.

Then we hugged.

I couldn't find the words to tell her then, but I wanted her to know that no matter what she might think, she could count on one thing—and that was me.

19
It's How Much You've Lived

The next couple of days flew by. Laura had a couple of appointments and had to do an interview, so we didn't get to see each other much. And then it was Saturday. It was our last full day in Wisconsin and my final day with Laura. It also happened to be Aunt Karen's fiftieth birthday, so Uncle Jim had planned a huge birthday blowout at Lake Winnebago.

"It'll just be a small gathering—only a hundred of my closest friends and enemies," Aunt Karen joked.

I wasn't exactly thrilled about spending my last day with Laura this way, with a hundred other people. I was already bummed that we would have to say good-bye; I didn't have a lot of patience for a stupid birthday party, too.

But I had no idea what a magical day it would turn out to be. It started with Uncle Jim waking Brad and me up at 7:30. He ordered us into the kitchen, where we helped him fix a surprise breakfast in bed for Aunt Karen. Soon, we were cracking eggs, frying bacon, pouring out pancake batter, and making coffee. Uncle Jim was totally organized. He had been the company cook in Vietnam and expertly directed us through every step:

"Watch the egg shells, make sure there're no lumps in the pancakes, and whatever you boys do, don't bang any pans or drop anything. If she wakes up and smells food, she'll be onto us like a dog on a pork chop."

Then the three of us carried trays into the bedroom, where on Uncle Jim's cue, we sang "Happy Birthday." Aunt Karen sat up in bed, rubbed her eyes, and smiled.

"Holy crap, there's enough food here to feed two armies. What're you trying to do, kill me?"

Uncle Jim sat next to Aunt Karen, and Brad and I sat at the edge of the bed. We passed all the food around, and it was the most fun I'd had eating breakfast.

"So," I asked Aunt Karen, "what's it like being the big five-o?"

"How the hell would I know? I'm not claiming a day over 42. Age is only a state of mind, kiddo. Besides, it's not about how old you are, it's about how much you've lived. And I've lived a little, let me tell you."

"Please, no details—they're still minors!" Uncle Jim said. "Why don't we open the presents?"

Uncle Jim gave Aunt Karen a beautiful turquoise necklace. She seemed blown away. "I'll thank you for this later—privately." Brad and I cracked up, and Uncle Jim actually blushed. Brad got Aunt Karen a new yoga mat that she loved. But it was my gift that really got her to laugh.

The day before, Uncle Jim and I'd gone to a shop in town, and I'd found the perfect T-shirt: an image of an ornery-looking cow with a funny caption that read WISCONSIN: A MOOVING EXPERIENCE.

I paid extra to have them print up a new one, but with

my own original caption. The cow was now saying, "WE'RE DEAD MEAT: ANDY'S DRIVING!"

Aunt Karen unfolded the T-shirt and burst out laughing. "This is hysterical! I love it." She gave me a big hug, then slipped under the covers and came up wearing my T-shirt. "I'll cherish it forever, Andy."

"Hey, what about my yoga mat?" Brad asked.

"My *ass* will cherish *that* forever." She hugged Brad. "Thank you, all of you. Now get out of here 'cause I have to get ready for some serious partying!"

❖

She wasn't kidding. We arrived at Lake Winnebago around 11:00 a.m., and I couldn't believe the scene. People were pouring out of cars and trucks, and they headed toward the grassy shoreline. The guests were carrying coolers, tents, musical instruments, and volleyballs, and they were wearing every imaginable type of swimsuit. It was like the whole town had turned out for Aunt Karen.

Soon the lakefront had turned into a festival. There were barbecues going everywhere, drinks were flowing freely, small groups were playing music, and people were dancing. There was a caricature artist and even a fortune teller.

People were swimming in the lake, and a few boats pulled water-skiers. There was so much going on, it was hard to know what to do first.

"Now, these people know how to party," Brad said. "Come on. Let's learn how to water-ski."

"Maybe later," I said, looking toward the parking lot, where I saw the green SUV pull in.

"I hear ya," Brad said, with a knowing smile.

I ran over to greet Laura. She looked totally hot in a T-shirt and long flowered skirt, her hair flowing beneath a Green Bay Packers cap.

"Hey, you," she said, as we hugged.

"You look . . . great!"

"You don't look so bad yourself."

"Why didn't you tell me my aunt knew all of Wisconsin?"

"Your aunt rocks. She could be mayor if she wanted."

"I don't doubt it."

I helped Laura's mom take their stuff to the lakefront, then Aunt Karen came over and threw her arms around Mrs. Kearns.

"I'm so glad you're both here."

"Wouldn't miss it for anything," Mrs. Kearns said.

"Happy birthday, cool lady," Laura said.

Aunt Karen dropped down to her knees to give Laura a kiss, then looked up at Laura's mom. "And how about these two, huh?" Laura and I both rolled our eyes in unison.

"Andy's the sweetest boy. He's really so adorable," Laura's mom said.

"Yeah, he gets that from me," Aunt Karen cackled.

"I think this is where we get off," I said, pushing Laura's chair toward the lake.

"Thank you," Laura said. "What is it with adults who talk about you like you're not even there?"

"I know. It's, like, so lame."

Laura and I made our first stop at the caricaturist. The artist was a chubby man in his thirties who wore a purple beret. He sat at an easel and drew furiously with several different colors of chalk. I sat down in a chair, and Laura rolled up next to me. I put my arm around her, and she leaned her head toward mine.

"That's perfect," the artist said. "Love really brings out the glow in everyone."

Laura and I glanced at each other and instantly burst out laughing. No one had ever mentioned the "L" word in describing us before, and we were both a little embarrassed.

After an awkward silence, wondering who was glowing more, I said, "I can't believe I'm leaving tomorrow."

"Hey, you're not gonna get all mushy on me now, are you?" Laura said.

"Nah. Don't worry."

"What time are you flying out tomorrow?"

"Eleven-thirty," I said.

"I'll be long gone by then."

Laura was leaving the next day, too. She had a very early flight out of Madison to Chicago, then she was flying to Boston. She had a concert there the next night.

"So we've got, like, just a few hours left together," she said.

We sat there in silence, letting this fact sink in. A few minutes later, the artist turned the easel to show us the finished sketch. "Here we are."

"I love it! It's so fantastic!" Laura said.

"Uh . . . well, not exactly," I said, a little hesitantly.

"What do you mean, Andy? It's great. You look totally cute."

"My ears are way too big. Who, outside of the elephant kingdom, has ears like that?" I protested.

"You'll grow into them," the artist said. "It's a caricature, kid. Things have to be a bit exaggerated."

"Couldn't you have exaggerated my biceps?" I asked.

"Lighten up, Andy. It's perfect. Can I have it, please? I have the perfect frame for it," Laura said.

"Sure, but I get visitation rights."

"Deal."

As we left the artist, it was getting hotter out and more people were in the lake.

"God, the water looks amazing," Laura said. "Andy, would you do something for me?"

"Sure."

"Would you take me swimming?"

"'Course, no problem."

"Well, there is a little problem. I haven't been swimming in public since I was four. I mean, I have to put a swimsuit on and, well . . . I think maybe I should warn you about my legs."

"What do you mean?" I asked, a little confused.

"They look ugly. And they're almost not like real legs anymore."

I wasn't exactly sure what she was saying, but I wasn't going to let anything stop us. "Laura, I'd love to go swimming with you."

With her mom's help, Laura got dressed in a changing tent. She rolled out in her chair, wearing a one-piece blue swimsuit with a beach towel draped over her legs. Her mother didn't look too happy.

"Laura, are you sure you want to do this? You haven't been swimming in . . . "

"Yes, Mom, I *really* want to do this. And I'm going to be fine. Andy's an all-state swimmer."

This was news to me; I suck at swimming because I choke when water gets up my nose, and it almost always does. But I flashed my best all-state swimmer smile, probably fooling no one.

Laura rolled across the grassy area, up to the edge of the sand. Then she looked up, and she stopped.

"Sorry, Andy. This model doesn't have four-wheel drive. How strong are you?"

"Hey, I'm an all-state swimmer, remember."

"I don't need Michael Phelps, just a cute guy who can carry me to the water . . . or you." She laughed.

Laura took the towel off her legs and threw it over her shoulder. Even though she'd warned me, what I saw was pretty shocking.

Her legs were extremely thin, atrophied from more than 10 years of inactivity. White from not being exposed to sunlight, they also had little shape, with no muscle development or tone. Compared to Laura's upper body, they didn't seem to belong there.

Sitting there so exposed, Laura couldn't have been more naked. But she sure had plenty of guts.

"It's not as bad as it looks," she said. "I've got so much less to shave." I smiled, but she'd seen my surprise, even though I'd tried hard not to react.

Then Laura raised her arms to me, and I bent down. Lifting her out of the chair, I carried her to the water. I couldn't believe how light she was.

We waded in, and I shivered, but Laura wasn't in the water yet. "Whoa, this water's pretty cold," I said through clenched teeth.

"Duh, it's a Wisconsin lake, Andy. This isn't some wuss California ocean. Now, we both know there's really only one way to do this, right?"

"Right . . . I guess." Then, holding her tight, I took a few steps and submerged us. Laura came up screaming.

"It's freezing, you maniac!"

"Duh, it's a Wisconsin lake, Laura." We bobbed around in the water, and Laura held on tight. And I didn't mind a bit.

"Okay," she said. "Let me go."

"You sure?" I asked, wide-eyed.

"Yeah. What's the worst that could happen? If I drown, you get custody of the caricature."

"I'll take really good care of it, I promise," I said. Then Laura nodded, indicating that she was ready. I quickly glanced back at the shore at her mom, who was watching anxiously from her towel. Then we both let go.

Laura tried to dog paddle with her arms, pumping them furiously below the water. She kept herself up for several seconds, then quickly sank below the surface. I grabbed her arm, and she popped up, smiling and out of breath.

"Wow! It's much harder than the therapy pool. I'm so totally out of shape. It feels great, though! I love it!"

She held on to me and floated on her back. Nearby, powerboats were pulling water-skiers, and one boat was tugging a kid in a big inner tube. We watched him ride by, then she got that look in her eye.

"I want to try that, Andy. We *have* to try it!"

"I'm there."

I loved Laura's sense of adventure. Her mom, however, did not. She was afraid this ride might be dangerous. As we worked on convincing her, Uncle Jim came to our aid.

The boat owner, Sam, was a friend of his from when he first moved to town. Uncle Jim promised Laura's mom that Sam was very careful and that no one had ever been hurt when Sam pulled them in the inner tube.

After a lot of reassurance, and when she saw how excited Laura was, Mrs. Kearns finally gave in.

Laura got back in her chair, and we made our way over to the dock, where Sam gave us a couple of life jackets. Then I carried Laura to the edge of the dock and jumped in, still holding her tight. We got into the tube and wrapped our arms around the sides, then Sam gave me the plastic handle of a long towrope and told me to hang on tight. If we got into trouble or wanted to stop, all I had to do was let go of the rope.

"You ready?" I asked Laura.

She wrapped her free arm around my shoulder and said, "I am now."

I gave Sam a thumbs-up, and he pulled away from the dock. He drove slowly at first, gradually speeding up until the rope was taut. Then he picked up speed.

Gliding through the cold lake water was an awesome sensation. The boat's wake sprayed in our faces, and the inner tube bounced along the surface, gliding from side to side. When the boat sped up really fast, we were actually out of the water, riding up in the air. Laura screamed with delight the whole time, and I laughed just from watching her glee.

When we finally slowed down and circled back to the dock, Laura threw her arms around me.

"That was the most fun I've had—probably ever. Thank you so much, Andy."

Laura looked as happy as I'd ever seen her. Then I remembered something Aunt Karen had said that made sense now: it really *is* about how much you've lived. Like my aunt, Laura had that gift—an amazing spirit. She wasn't afraid to go for it. And lucky for me, it's contagious.

20

It Sucks to Say Good-bye

I felt totally alive after our inner-tube ride; all my senses were cranked to the max. This amazing euphoria replaced my earlier gloom about leaving, making me grateful to be with Laura. I wanted to enjoy every minute we had.

The rest of our day flew. We made the rounds and sampled all kinds of stuff to eat, including Uncle Jim's famous grilled sausage and peppers, which were awesome.

People kept coming over to Laura, telling her they'd seen her perform or had her CD. A few even asked for her autograph. As modest as she was, Laura was a big star in this little town.

Later in the afternoon, two hearses pulled into the parking lot, both honking their horns. Bones and his jazz band unpacked their instruments and set up a makeshift stage near the lake.

They brought an electric piano, and Bones invited Laura to sit in with them. Everyone gathered around, and many began to dance. Even Brad, who hates dancing, boogied with a hot-looking older girl.

Aunt Karen came up to me with a drink in her hand, and by now was feeling no pain. "You think you're getting out of here alive without dancing with me?"

"I wouldn't even try," I said as she led me toward the other dancers. I know I shouldn't have been surprised, but she was graceful and light on her feet, shaking everything that shook.

I did my best just to move with the beat, being about as adept at dancing as I was at quantum physics. But dancing with Aunt Karen, I couldn't help but get caught up in the moment. I began making moves I'd never done before, including a 360 turn.

"Look at you! Nice move there, Andy. There's hope for you yet, kid."

Laura gave me a thumbs-up from the stage, and when the music ended, I walked Aunt Karen to a shady tree, where she tried to catch her breath.

"This is a very cool party," I said.

"Yeah, isn't it something? And it's so much more special having you and Brad here."

"I want to thank you . . . for everything. I'll never forget this trip."

"It's been a kick for me, too, Andy," Aunt Karen said. "It's been terrific getting to know you guys."

"You, too! You're the coolest adult I've ever met."

"Why, thank you, Andy. That's because most of the time, I think I'm still 19. Unfortunately, my chins think they're 60." Then she cackled that laugh of hers and gave me a big sweaty hug.

Suddenly, our conversation was interrupted by loud static and a screeching sound coming from near the band.

It was Uncle Jim, on stage with a microphone. "Can I have your attention, please?" Everyone quieted down.

"I want to thank you all for coming out to celebrate Karen's big birthday. I've been with this lady for 32 years now, and she is definitely one of a kind."

With that, everyone cheered. Aunt Karen took a bow, almost falling over.

"This amazing woman can quote Shakespeare, dye her hair three different colors in one day, teach a dog to give the finger, and make a killer margarita. Of course, the margarita's for breakfast."

By now, Jim had everyone laughing. "I could go on and on, but she's getting old now and may forget this toast. So let's all raise a glass to Karen, the woman who taught me how to kick life's butt!"

Now someone brought out a huge birthday cake, glowing with 50 candles. Bones led us in "Happy Birthday," and I led a slightly teary Aunt Karen over to the stage.

"See what you've all made me do? I haven't cried since George Dubya was re-elected. I know I'm so lucky to have so many good friends. 'Course, right now, I don't recognize any of you. And who was that handsome stranger giving the toast?" she asked, as everyone laughed.

"Thank you all so much for being here and for being in my life. I especially want to thank my nephews, Brad and Andy, who came all the way from planet California. Now, mark your calendars, 'cause we're all doing this again 50 years from now, on my hundredth birthday!"

Everyone cheered and surrounded Aunt Karen as I made my way to Laura.

"That was pretty great, wasn't it?" she said.

"Yeah. They're both so cool."

As the sun began setting on the lake, its rays turned the water purple and orange. I wheeled Laura over to a secluded spot offering a great view, then lifted her out of her chair, settling her onto the blanket I'd spread on the grass.

We held hands as birds dove into the lake, leaving ripples in their wake. The joyous sounds of the party became background noise of music and conversation. We could hear Aunt Karen's occasional cackle as we sat there, taking it all in.

"It was a perfect day," Laura said.

"Yeah. It really *was* perfect."

Another bird swooped down with a splash.

"I've always wanted to fly like that," Laura said.

"Yeah. It'd be great just to be able to go anywhere with that kind of freedom."

"The feeling of the wind in your face."

"Being able to get to school in, like, six seconds."

"Yeah, and on the way, you can drop little surprises on people you can't stand."

I laughed. "You're so twisted."

"Yeah? Then what does that say about you, hanging out with me?"

"It says I have excellent taste in women," I said.

And then I kissed her. This was more than just a top-of-the-Ferris-wheel first kiss like the other night. This was a serious, passionate kiss, a kiss that wasn't interrupted because the ride ended. It was like we'd been kissing for years.

Finally, we came up for air.

"Where'd you learn to kiss like that?" she asked.

"From you, and I don't want to know where you learned it." She laughed.

"I can't believe how lucky I am . . . meeting you like I did," she said.

"Yeah, me, too. Life is so weird sometimes."

She put her head on my shoulder, and we watched the last sliver of orange sun dip below the horizon. As I inhaled Laura's perfume mixed with the scent of the nearby pine trees, I thought about how we'd gotten together and how random it all seemed.

It had all lined up so perfectly. First, Hawaii went up in smoke. Then we got shipped off to Wisconsin. And then I bumped into Laura—well, technically, I bumped into the pole while I flirted with Laura. And she just happened to be in the parking lot at that exact moment when I was there. Then what about Uncle Jim having her as a guest on his show, and Aunt Karen and Clyde practically dragging me to the station to meet her? I guess the planets all aligned just right, or whatever.

But as fateful as it might have been, I realized that Aunt Karen was right again. If I hadn't gotten off my butt and gotten out of the house, I never would have met this amazing girl. That's where things actually happen—in the real world, not on Facebook or on TV.

My pondering was interrupted by a voice: "Honey, it's getting late." Laura's mom had found us and was there with her things all gathered up. She looked at us apologetically. "You have a very early flight tomorrow, and we still have to go home and pack."

"Okay, Mom. Can you give us a couple of minutes?" Mrs. Kearns nodded.

"It was great meeting you, Andy." She walked over, and I got up to hug her.

"Great meeting you, too, Mrs. Kearns." She kissed my cheek and walked away.

Laura and I were alone, and I returned to her on the blanket. It seemed to get eerily quiet.

"Guess this is it," she said.

"I guess so. I'm going to call you as soon as I land in San Francisco."

"I hope so. We can talk every day—that's if you want to," she said, seeming a bit unsure.

"Of course I want to," I said. "And we'll see each other again. Maybe I can come back before school starts."

"That'd be great," she said. "Because once we're in school . . . "

She didn't have to finish. We were both thinking the same thing. It wasn't going to be easy. Sure, with cell phones, texting, Facebook, we could definitely stay in touch. But as far as seeing her, those green eyes and that great smile . . . that certain look she'd get when she was about to do something crazy—I was really going to miss all that.

We kissed once more and held tight, neither wanting to let go. Then she pulled away and forced herself to smile.

"I guess I'd better get going. Can you help me to my wheels?"

I lifted her off the blanket and back into the chair. She took my hand and smiled.

"I had so much fun with you."

"Me, too," I said. "You're like . . . you're like no one else I've ever met."

Laura smiled. I got behind her wheelchair, but she waved me off. She knew it would be easier—for both of us—for her to leave on her own.

"Have a safe trip," she said.

"You, too. Got my cell number, right?"

"I tattooed it onto my chest. I'll show it to you next time you're here. That way, you'll *have* to come back." It was so like her to leave me laughing.

Then Laura motioned me back to her. As I leaned down, she took off the Green Bay Packers cap and put it on my head. She sat there for a moment, just looking at me.

"I want to remember you just like this." Tears welled up in her eyes.

"You're not gonna get all mushy on me now, are you?" I asked.

"Nah. That's not how I roll."

And with that, she turned her chair around and headed for the parking lot.

I stood there watching until she disappeared into a sea of partygoers.

I missed her already.

21

Going Home

I picked up my last shirt, stuffed it into the suitcase, and slowly pulled the zipper closed. This was it. I'd be flying home soon.

I looked in the mirror and adjusted Laura's Green Bay Packers cap. Man, did I look lousy—exactly like I felt.

My throat was tight, my stomach was in knots, and a sleepless night had left me groggy and light-headed. I had never felt so bad about leaving a place. And it wasn't just because of Laura. I was becoming really tight with my aunt and uncle and was even getting into the rural thing—horse crap and all.

Okay, I admit it. As much as I really loved Aunt Karen and Uncle Jim, it really *was* all about Laura. Yesterday was about as perfect as a day could be, and it just made me want to be with her even more.

But as much as I told myself I'd see her again, I couldn't shake this one terrible thought: What if we *really* never saw each other again?

"Dude, we gotta jam." It was Brad, snapping me back to reality. He grabbed my suitcase.

"I can get it," I said.

"You look kind of wiped out. I'll take it for you."

Boy, this was not the same Brad I left San Francisco with. It was like our whole relationship had changed in just a few weeks. Right now, I was his equal, but I wondered how long it would last.

I followed Brad into the living room, where Uncle Jim and Aunt Karen were standing by our luggage. Aunt Karen was wearing the T-shirt I'd given her for her birthday, and I smiled when I saw it.

"I guess we better be goin'," Uncle Jim said. "It's been a real treat having you guys here with us."

"It was awesome. You made it really special. Thanks for everything," Brad said. "Especially for rescuing me on the side of the road when I lost my mind."

"Don't mention it," Aunt Karen said. "I lost my mind years ago, and I still haven't found it." She gave him a hug. "But you sure did scare the hell out of me, Bradley."

Brad smiled and shrugged.

Then Aunt Karen turned to me. "And you. You didn't do too badly here, did you?"

"I guess not. You guys have been amazing. This has been the best two weeks of my life. And Uncle Jim, thanks for introducing me to Laura."

Then I turned to Aunt Karen. "And thanks for making me go meet her."

Clyde barked. Maybe he was feeling left out. "I'm not forgetting you, boy. You're *so* easy to talk to." I bent down, and he licked my face.

"And who almost got killed just so you could learn to drive?" Aunt Karen pointed to her T-shirt.

"That was definitely above and beyond. No offense, but I'm using a different driving teacher when I go for my actual license."

"I hope she's got a lot of life insurance."

I went over to Aunt Karen and gave her a big hug, letting her totally crush me. Then I hugged Uncle Jim, who was just as sincere—but a lot less dangerous.

"You boys have an open invite to come back any time you want," Uncle Jim said.

"If it was up to me," I said, "I'd be coming back tomorrow."

"You can't, kid," Aunt Karen said. "It's gonna take me a month just to restock the refrigerator."

❖

"Flight 200 to Chicago is now boarding at Gate 19." That was us. Brad had called Mom and Dad, who were already back home. He let them know our flight was leaving on time.

"Safe trip, guys," Uncle Jim said. He shook our hands. Aunt Karen put her arms around Brad and me, reeling us into a three-way hug.

"Tell your folks that they raised two terrific sons," she said.

"You tell them that next time they ground us," Brad quipped.

"So, are you going to call your old aunt once in a while?"

"Of course," I said. "And if you want, you can get on Facebook and we can talk over that."

"Don't hold your breath, kiddo. I'm still learning how to use call waiting."

They called our flight again, and we picked up our carry-on bags. Aunt Karen planted a wet kiss on each of us, then we walked through the gate. I was really going to miss these people.

Once we were on the plane, we came to our row in coach. Without hesitation, Brad gave me the window seat. I was starting to enjoy this new Brad, and I made a mental note to ask for his room when we got home.

As the plane's engines revved, the finality of leaving really hit me. My throat got tight again, and I felt myself choking up.

"You okay, Andy?"

"Yeah, I guess."

"Dude, you really got it bad," Brad said, patting me on the shoulder.

"I know."

"I'm going to help you get through this," Brad said. Now, this was too much. My brother had morphed into Dr. Phil.

A few minutes later, we were over the bright morning clouds. I stared at them, deep in thought. My girlfriend was on a plane, too, going in the opposite direction. Was she looking out at her clouds and thinking about me?

Wait a minute. I just called her my girlfriend. When did that happen? *Was* Laura my girlfriend? And could she actually be my girlfriend, even though we'd be 2,000 miles apart?

I decided that the answer to both questions was yes. It

was about time I had a girlfriend. I even tried the word out in my mind: *My girlfriend's in Wisconsin. It's a present from my girlfriend.* I really liked how it sounded.

This instantly made me feel better, and I decided not to dwell on us being apart. Instead, I closed my eyes and pictured all my great moments with Laura: The first time I saw her in that car—that hair, those eyes. Watching her flying down the bowling lane in her wheelchair. Playing blues piano in a funeral home. Posing as a mannequin in a department store. Kissing me on top of the Ferris wheel (my favorite). I pictured the absolute joy on her face as we glided over the lake in the inner tube. . . .

Brad jabbed at my arm. "Dude, you've got, like, the biggest smile on your face. What's so funny?"

"Nothing." I quietly calmed myself down.

Then a flight attendant came up the aisle and stopped at our row.

"Andy Crenshaw?"

"Yes."

"A passenger in first class found your photo I.D."

"My photo I.D.?"

The only photo I.D. I had was my lame student I.D. card. I reached for my wallet, but the flight attendant was reaching over and handing me something. It was a rolled-up sheet of white paper. I slipped off the rubber band and opened it.

To my utter confusion, it was the caricature of Laura and me. There was a Post-it note attached: *You can't get rid of me that easily, big ears.*

Then it hit me.

"She's on the plane!" I said to Brad.

"I know." He was smiling devilishly.

"You knew about this?"

"Yeah. We all did."

"Holy crap!" People began looking up from their magazines, and Brad began to laugh.

"Come on, I'll take you up there," the flight attendant said.

My legs were shaky as I stood up. I could hardly breathe as I stumbled over Brad to get to the aisle. I grinned at every passenger along the way as I walked the 38 rows to first class.

The flight attendant parted the curtains, and there she was. Sitting with her mother in the first row, Laura wore a killer grin that said "What took you so long?"

"What are you doing here, on my plane?"

"Oh, so now you own this plane?" she said, cool as ever.

"How . . . what . . . when . . . ?" I couldn't even form the questions that buzzed around in my mind.

"My concert in Boston was cancelled, so we exchanged it for a gig in San Francisco. I'll be spending a whole week there."

Laura's mom was now out of her seat, motioning for me to take it.

"I don't believe this," I sputtered. "Is this really happening?"

Laura's mom hugged me. "Sit here, Andy. I'll go back and take your seat."

"You don't have to do that, Mrs. Kearns."

"I want to," she said. "It's really no bother."

"Yes, it is. You'll have to spend four hours with my brother Brad."

"Those are the sacrifices we make for our children." She grabbed her bag and walked up the aisle. Then I sat down in the big leather seat next to Laura. She threw her arms around me, and we kissed.

We could hear an audible "Awww" from the other people in first class. One couple even applauded.

"You're going to show me every square inch of San Francisco," Laura said, taking out a guidebook and thumbing through it.

"I want to go over the Golden Gate Bridge and see Fisherman's Wharf, and we have to go to Alcatraz! I hear it's totally cool, and I want to ride a cable car down that crooked street, and . . . "

She went on and on, but I didn't hear a word. I just sat there looking at her, wondering how I ever got so lucky.

I'll never adequately describe how happy I was, sitting on that flight with Laura. Let's just say I could have flown home without the plane.

Aknowledgments

Writing can be somewhat intimidating. Luckily, I had a few people who helped me along the way. I'm so grateful to my family, Susan, Kevin, and Eric, for reading earlier chapters of this book and encouraging me to keep going. Without their love and support, *The Summer I Got a Life* would still be an idea stuck in the back of my head.

I'd like to thank Alison Picard for finding the right place for this book. My publisher, Evelyn Fazio, worked closely with me on this novel, and I am grateful for her patience and insights.